DREAM HUNTERS

NAZIMA PATHAN

DREAM HUNTERS

SIMON & SCHUSTER

First published in Great Britain in 2024 by Simon & Schuster UK Ltd

Text copyright © 2024 Nazima Pathan
Illustration copyright © 2024 Geraldine Rodríguez

1 3 5 7 9 10 8 6 4 2

Simon & Schuster UK Ltd
1st Floor, 222 Gray's Inn Road
London WC1X 8HB

www.simonandschuster.co.uk
www.simonandschuster.com.au
www.simonandschuster.co.in

Simon & Schuster Australia, Sydney
Simon & Schuster India, New Delhi

A CIP catalogue record for this book is available from the British Library.

PB ISBN 978-1-3985-3188-8
eBook ISBN 978-1-3985-3190-1
eAudio ISBN 978-1-3985-3189-5

This book is a work of fiction. Names, characters, places and incidents are either
the product of the author's imagination or are used fictitiously. Any resemblance
to actual people living or dead, events or locales is entirely coincidental.

Typeset by Palimpsest Book Production Ltd, Falkirk, Stirlingshire

Printed and Bound in the UK using 100% Renewable Electricity
at CPI Group (UK) Ltd

MIX
Paper | Supporting
responsible forestry
FSC® C171272

For Pierre, Zahra and Léon

Open your eyes,
For this world is only a dream.

Rumi

Prologue

It was midnight when they found him.

Whirling, churning, simmering. The angry dream threads raged against their confinement in the glass that contained them.

Hidden in the shadows, the intruder uncapped and inverted the vial, unleashing a cascade of nightmares. Expertly distilled, and angry as bears, they slithered over each other, fighting their way out of the dirty, grey bottle. Hissing and cursing, they dripped like an oil slick onto the soft rug at the foot of a wide mahogany bed. They crawled and curled across the tufted wool. Coiling snake-like around the carved wooden legs of the bed frame, they closed in on the sleeping form of Ganipal the Third, king of Ratnagar, loved by his people and feared by his enemies.

These were fierce dream threads, and they sought their target hungrily, lifting their tips to sense their way. Soon enough they reached the sleeping form of the king, huddled on his soft, silk-lined mattress in fitful slumber.

Above the door a clock chimed twelve times, its hands coming together in a fateful embrace and, as they did, a dark shadow of nightmares enveloped the king. The ghostly-green threads melted into his mind, whispering threats of pain, suffering and death.

Submerged in the sudden terror of a thousand spectres, the king was powerless to escape, powerless to wake. All he could do was toss and moan.

The intruder crept to a mirror behind the door and took out a long, thin object. The dark, ebony stem was tipped by a weather-worn metal hook. It sparked as it was swept in a circle across the looking glass, transforming the mirror into a rippling liquid through which a hidden world came into view. After a glance towards the sleeping, struggling king, the intruder softly stepped through the mirror and out of the room.

The old king's breath came fast as distorted visions

of his past and present taunted him. The nightmares clawed in, crushing his hope, flaying his mind and squeezing his soul. Weak as a hare in the grip of a fox's closing jaw, the king readied himself for the end.

But this time, the nightmare was not dosed to kill.

Next time, they would finish the job.

CHAPTER ONE

The Dream Hunt

In the Citadel, we hunt.

Dreams are our prey. If we catch them before they melt into moonlight, they can be recycled and sold for great profit. My family has been hunting dreams for generations. Capturing them as they slip away, and storing them in a soaring, magnificent library. Blue glass bottles on bulging shelves glint with promise, their precious contents conserved and classified, ready to be cast in a new story, for a new mind. The dreamers dream and the sleepers pay us well.

As much as the Library of Forgotten Dreams is the brains of the Citadel, the Hall of Mirrors is its beating heart. A circular, windowless building where we work in shifts, scouring the globe for forgotten dreams. We hunt in pairs. One to navigate the hunt, the other to catch our prey, snaring dream threads on long-stemmed hooks and bottling them away.

I jostle through the queue to reach my fellow hunter, Rafi. Street urchin, pickpocket, fighter were all labels he had in his former life, but here in the Citadel he is just one of many students making their way from hunters to curators and designers of dreams.

The librarian gazes at me over the top of her glasses. She has soft eyes, clouded by dreams she has gathered and sorted over many years, but her brief nod betrays a flash of recognition. Behind her there is a rack of keys, ready to unlock gateways to the dreams we will hunt tonight.

'Name?' She taps her manicured fingers on the desk.

'Malou, Mimi.' She knows who I am, but I play the game. I've attended night hunts since before I could even walk.

The old woman sniffs, slipping one of the keys across the desk. The tag has co-ordinates scratched on it in golden ink.

Latitude 27° 28' 10". Longitude 70° 37' 18".

I close my hand around the cold metal. The key is heavier than it looks and is inscribed with charms. Rafi paces ahead of me, diving into the atlas when we reach our station, while I insert the key into a lock crafted into the frame of our looking glass. As I turn the key a series of *clunks* signals our destination is set and the portal is ready. Our reflection fades and shifting shadows come into view.

On the other side of the mirror, the sky is a dark pool of ink smattered with a shimmering belt of stars. It is perfectly cloudless, perfectly clear, perfect for dream hunting. Rafi sinks the lever controlling our looking glass, and our viewpoint drops closer to the ground. Waves of sand dunes drift across a desolate landscape.

My dream creature, Lalu, flutters around my head. Excited and anxious, her hummingbird wings are a rich azure blue; she has flecks of gold and pink at the nape of her tiny neck.

'It's a desert,' says Rafi.

'The sand's a clue, I suppose.'

'So smart.' He rotates the lever and we pan across the scene on the other side of the looking glass, 'The Thar Desert. It's in the north of India.'

'You've been?'

He shakes his head. 'This is about as far from Mumbai as you can get,' he says.

As we scour across the sand, I wonder how we will find any living creature, let alone a dream.

'There!' Rafi zooms our looking glass down towards a clump of red and orange in the distance, the dying embers of a campfire. In its dim light I spy a cluster of tents and slumbering camels. A guard rests his head against a dusty stack of travelling bags. He is motionless, but now and then his sleepy head slips to one side and he stirs.

'Him?' I ask, but Rafi shakes his head.

'The camel?' I snigger and he punches my arm.

'Look.' He points to the bottom-right corner of the looking glass.

All I see is a tent swathed in darkness. 'You sure?'

Rafi bites his lip as he steers our looking glass across the camp, the amber firelight fading into darkness. He's not done so well the last couple of times. While he has a real skill for spotting dreams, he isn't so good at reeling them in. It needs a delicate touch and losing one is worse than never finding it. Three failed hunts mean being kicked out of the programme.

'See it now?' Rafi points to a wisp of light slithering

out of the tent. It's a soft, speckled, golden colour and undulates, coiling around on itself. Its tip wiggles playfully as if it's sniffing the night air. I know that dreams start to unfurl as the memory of them fades, but this one is still a perfect helix, as if it has only just slipped out of the dreamer's mind.

I run my finger across the classification table in my copy of *A Beginner's Guide to Dream Hunting*.

Colour: gold . . . Shape: helical . . . Movement: playful . . .

'Fresh grade one dream fragment,' I say. 'Rare as flying horses.'

Lalu watches from my shoulder, her wings quivering every now and then in excitement. Rafi's dream creature is a chiffchaff. Like her human, Mithi is good-natured, often hungry and chatters constantly. She settles on the top of our looking glass, warbling and waggling her tail while I uncap a bottle to trap the dream thread once we reel it in. As we steer towards it, a drift of wind puffs the thread further away from us. It quivers, threatening to unfurl.

'I'm on it, Mimi!' Rafi moves the lever but forces it too hard. The glass jerks and we lose sight of the camp.

'Nice and slow.' I grab the controls, trying to

re-centre. I zoom up and guide the portal back to the original co-ordinates. Nothing.

Then I spot it—

Yes! We can fix this.

We move in fast. This time, I steer. The dream sparkles as it senses the mirror, and my insides turn into a spray of butterflies. Rafi holds his dream hook close to the glass and sweeps a circle across the surface, transforming it into a rippling silver liquid. As we move close to the portal, the chill night air in the desert makes goosebumps spring up on my arms.

'Move like a ghost,' I say.

I hold my breath as the wisp floats towards us. Rafi slides his dream-weaving hook through the mirror, twists his hand and catches a loop of dream onto it.

'Great, now pull it through,' I say. 'Nice and slow . . . you've got this.'

'I have?'

I nod and smile at him.

'Yes, I've got this,' he says.

He hasn't.

His hand shakes as a dream technician passes by.

He's nervous.

The dream quivers . . . Mithi flits around the mirror

and I shoo her away. Now is not the time for distraction, but it's too late. The golden dream thread slivers and shivers. My heart sinks as it unwinds and slips away, fluttering down through the sky on the other side of the looking glass. Down, unravelling and splintering into countless pieces until, *poof,* it's gone.

As if it never existed.

Sensing the dream has disappeared, the mirror portal starts to reset and solid glass closes in on Rafi's dream hook. By the time he tries to pull it out, the end of it is stuck, captured like the branch of a tree in a frozen lake.

He turns to me wide-eyed. 'It won't come out!'

I wipe my forehead. If we can find another dream, the portal will open and free the hook, but before I can reset the lock Rafi panics and pulls the stem of his hook.

'No, don't, it can't just . . .' The rest of my words melt into a horrified gasp as a crack appears in the mirror. Then another. Hundreds more appear, flourishing web-like across the surface of the mirror. Pieces of glass start to slip and fall away from the frame, clattering in thunderous symphony onto the stone floor of the Hall of Mirrors.

Children around us pause their hunts. The room burns with their whispered questions and their pitying, wondering gaze.

My face flushes red. 'Quick, let's clear this up.' I start to pick at the larger mirror fragments, but I know it's futile. The technicians monitor all our activity, and it won't be long before word reaches the top.

I clench my fists as I spot some of the other students, Deena Dilsay and her pig-headed friends, sniggering as Rafi looks for a brush to sweep away the glass, but we all stiffen when we hear her.

Click, clack.

She's coming.

Click, clack.

The other children jump back into their hunts and try to look busy, their attention focused on their own mirrors, not the fallen fragments of ours.

The footsteps get louder, and Aunt Moyna bustles in, trailed by her troop of dream technicians and a fluttering flock of dream creatures circling above them, ravens and rooks with an affinity for harsh dreams and cold feelings. They make a beeline for our station.

'I'll say it was me,' I say and clear my throat.

'No way,' Rafi whispers. 'I won't let you.'

I shake my head and push myself in front of him. Luckily, I'm half a head taller.

'*Hmmm* . . .' Aunt Moyna arrives at our station, kicking at broken shards of glass. She has her hair pulled into a tight bun, which makes her sharp, chiselled features even more severe.

'It's not what you think—' I start but Aunt Moyna raises her hand, and my stomach rolls over itself.

She leans over to pick up Rafi's fallen dream hook and, as she stands up, adjusts her glasses and reads the name at the end of the hook.

'Well, it comes as no surprise, Rafi. You've been trouble since I invited you into the Citadel.'

My aunt has always said orphans handle dreams better because they have no hopes or dreams of their own. That's why she has brought many in from beyond the Citadel, promising them a home and good food, but it comes with a liberal dose of discipline and fear. To be fair, most of them are as good at hunting as the older hunters born and bred here.

'It was my fault,' I say.

My aunt purses her lips and Rafi opens his mouth to say something, but I shake my head. Aunt Moyna took over from my father as head of the Library of Forgotten Dreams when my parents were imprisoned, so she's my guardian as well as my boss.

'You know very well, Mimi, that because you have no blood link to Rafi his hook would not respond to you.' She circles her hand across the scene before us. 'This incompetence is all the doing of your fellow dream hunter.'

'He's new. I should have taken control.'

Aunt Moyna ignores me and bends down, bringing her face level with Rafi's. Undeterred, he gives her a defiant stare. I touch his shoulder in warning, but he shrugs me off.

'Maybe being a common thief is all you were ever good for.'

Rafi scowls. 'I took care of myself.'

I reach out to calm him as one of the technicians grabs his arm. She has a distinctive white streak in her hair, like someone has run some chalk along it, but I take a step back when I see her badge:

Senior Supervisory Technician, Suri Ganatry.

Technicians are the supervisors of sadness, the harbingers of hate. Even Deena's smirk has stiffened to worry.

'Let me go!' Rafi wriggles and winces at the tightness of the grip on his arm, but Suri maintains her lobster-tight hold. Her raven shrieks with amusement.

'That's enough, Carab.' Aunt Moyna swipes at Suri's dream creature. As he flaps away, she turns her attention back to Rafi. 'Maybe you need a trip to the dream laboratory.'

A ripple of dread spreads through the hall. No one comes back the same after a trip to the dream laboratory.

'Aunt Moyna, please . . .' My throat is so dry I can barely speak.

I like Rafi. He is a little clumsy, but he tries his best, and even though he's smaller than me he fights back when some of the other kids call me a traitor like my parents.

My aunt lifts her hand up. 'You may release him, Suri.'

The woman relaxes her grip and Rafi pulls away, rubbing his shoulder and shooting dagger eyes at the technician.

'Now look,' says Aunt Moyna, 'the looking glass is a precious tool. A portal is not a toy to roam the world.' She turns to Rafi, eyebrows furrowed. 'Take this as a final warning. No more chances, no more excuses.' She takes out her notebook and scribbles a note in her tally.

Dream hunts are scored, and we just failed.

'Can I just say—' starts Rafi, but she holds up her hand to silence him.

'This looking glass will take months to repair.' Aunt Moyna steps on a fragment of broken glass and crushes it with her heel. 'We will find a spare, but you have quite a debt of dreams to repay.'

Lalu takes refuge in the nest of moss and leaves in my pocket. I stroke the soft feathers on the back of her neck to calm her down.

'You are better than this, Mimi,' says Aunt Moyna. 'Perhaps you should work with someone more accomplished?' She turns her head towards Deena then back to me and gives a slight nod.

I growl and shake my head, looking down as she *click-clack*s away with her retinue of technicians behind her. I'm no traitor, and there is no way I would give up on my best friend. Suri looks back and, as she catches my eye, her thin smile prickles my anger.

Trouble is closing in on Rafi, and where trouble goes, danger follows.

CHAPTER TWO

An Unusual Visitor

We make our way out of the hall into the market square, where noisy traders are selling food, fabrics and fine metal trinkets from their wooden stalls draped with vibrant silks and twinkling lights. The clamour and colour wash away some of my worries, and the scent of flatbreads tossed on open fires drives the rest down for a while.

Rafi offers the baker a coin from his pocket money and takes a freshly cooked flatbread. It is as big as a dinner plate and he tosses it from hand to hand as he rips it in two, offering me the slightly smaller portion and scoffing his share in two big mouthfuls.

'Hungry?' I smile and peck at my share, the charred dough still warm and yeasty.

Rafi laughs. 'Not too hungry to share. Thanks for helping with your aunt.'

'She just wants what's best for the Citadel.'

'She drives us too hard though.' Rafi's eyes darken as two ravens chase each other overhead. The harsh, silver dream threads within them give their feathers a malicious glint, and we linger under the shade of the baker's tent until they pass.

'If I get sent back home, we'll still be friends, won't we?'

'Let's not get to that point,' I say, but Rafi's words give me goose pimples.

We both know that return for the exiled is impossible. The centuries-old hilltop citadel I call home cannot be found on any map. Hidden from the outer world behind a spell of protection, only the invited may enter, and while some may find us by chance, most are turned away. Only the traders and buyers of dreams may enter by permit.

'I'm going to work on my dream-hooking skills tonight, Mimi,' says Rafi, breaking an awkward moment of silence.

I wrinkle my brow. 'How? You don't have your hook.'

A sly smile crosses Rafi's face. 'Once a pickpocket, always a pickpocket.' He pulls his dream hook out of his coat and twists his hand this way and that, as if he's coaxing a dream thread onto it. 'If only it was as easy as picking a lock.'

Rafi has tried to teach me his survival tricks as much as I've tried imparting the skills for dream hunting, but today my nerves are on edge. 'What were you thinking? The rules are clear: no hooks allowed home. If they see you . . .' I draw my finger theatrically across my neck and, though I say it in jest, the threat is real. Getting found out means eviction or, worse still, the dream laboratory.

Rafi stuffs the hook into his coat pocket.

'Okay, I just wanted to practise. You know, when I'm done, I'll be the best dream hunter around.'

'No chance,' I say. 'That spot is mine.'

'Yours *for now*!'

I point to the star on my lapel. 'Grade two dream hunter. Only two more levels till I can apply to be a library apprentice.'

'Fine! I'm going to be a dream threader then, making dreams instead of storing them.'

'Hey!' I shout, but Rafi is off, with Mithi dancing through the air behind him. He disappears into the crowds, heading back to the boys' dormitory.

Most folk – the traders, craftspeople and builders – live in houses and huts gathered lower down the hill, on the outskirts of the Citadel. But the hunters and handlers of dreams work round the clock, so our rooms are within the walls of the fortress, a short walk from the Library of Forgotten Dreams which dominates the skyline with its central dome. Glass bottles stacked on row upon row of shelves protect the dreams from degrading. They sparkle in the rays of the setting sun, splashing a rainbow of light out from the tall windows all along the length of the building.

An old woman drags a harp along the pathway. It's Madame Frenegonde, my music teacher. I help her to heave her instrument over the kerb and we pause near a hot drinks stall, where the warm scent of spiced tea wafts over us. She pulls her woollen shawl over her shoulders and adjusts the gold dream threader pin that holds it together.

'Ah, dear Mimi. You're looking pale. Would you care for something to drink?'

'Thank you, Madame, but I don't have time.' I need to get into the library before it closes.

The old woman frowns. 'You seem perturbed, little one.'

I surpassed her height many moons ago, but I bow my head with a smile. 'I'm worried for my friend Rafi.'

She nods with understanding, extending her hand out to let a soft, grey pigeon settle on her outstretched palm. It strikes me that, over the years, Madame Frenegonde and her dream creature have come to resemble each other. Careworn and curious.

'Chandi, my little pebble.' She strokes the pigeon's head. 'I think you will need to gift some of your dreams to young Mimi here.'

The bird opens its beak and coos. A soft silver thread falls out of its beak and floats towards me, erupting into flowers with bright pink petals which fizz as they melt into my skin. I sense my mother, a scent of vanilla and hot chocolate.

'This little one has plenty of dreams to fill my sleeping hours,' I say, holding my coat pocket open so that Lalu can peek out with her bright black eyes. Madame Frenegonde squeezes my arm and looks up to the horizon where grey clouds are gathering.

'Take care, my dear. There seems to be a storm on the way.'

She's right about the approaching storm in more ways than one.

'May your thoughts be luminous, Madame.' I nod to bid farewell.

Madame Frenegonde touches her forehead and smiles. 'Thank you, Mimi. May your dreams shine ever brightly.'

I trudge across the square to the library and sign the visitors' book. Dream threads jostle for my attention from the confines of their bottles as I pass them. Curious, playful, happy and cautious, they are a rainbow of colours, emotions and shapes. For now, I am seeking a place I have known for as long as I have lived. A faded yellow velvet sofa in the reading section of the library. It smells of books and dust and reminds me of the tales my aunt used to tell me about the outer world when I was young – when she was less busy and we had time for stories. I long for the old days, but her responsibilities are like giant hands, grabbing her away from me.

I curl myself into a tight knot in the gap behind the sofa. My plan is a simple one but involves sneaking into Aunt Moyna's office, so I wait, barely breathing, until the main entrance doors swing shut with a tired groan.

In the silence that follows, I poke my head out to

check the path is clear, but as I untangle my legs to stand up, I hear the neigh of horses and pounding hooves coming across the market square. From the window behind I see two men draped in scarlet cloaks and white turbans unstrap themselves from their horses, tall steeds with glistening, ebony-black hides. Clad in sparkling, gilded armour, these are no merchant horses, and like their riders they hold their heads high and flare their nostrils, as if the scents and sights of our working, trading citadel insult their privileged sensibilities. The thrum of the marketplace slows as people stop and stare. A cobbler stands up and nudges his apprentice, pointing at the men's polished leather boots and golden spurs.

One man, the older one, jumps off the horse outside the doorway of the library.

'Take the animals and feed them,' he says to his companion. His voice is deep and powerful, and he knows the impact of it as the other man scuttles away, head down. As the older man strides to the library entrance, a gust of wind catches his sumptuous silk cloak and it floats like a damask rose petal behind him. The man wrinkles his pointy nose, adjusts his turban and knocks three times on the library door.

Click, clack.

I peek out from my hiding place to see my aunt rushing to the entrance. She must have been expecting this visitor: her hair is loose, and she has cast off her white technician's coat.

Aunt Moyna grabs onto the long handles and pulls open the heavy doors.

'Jamal,' she says, 'you're back sooner than I expected.'

The man bows his head, and with a curt smile he enters the library and looks around. I edge back and keep a hand on Lalu, who is fidgeting in my pocket.

'Madame Moyna, my master wants something stronger. To finish the job,' says Jamal.

Ordinary visitors gasp in wonder at the colour and majesty of the library, but this visitor is different. No stopping to marvel at the frescoed ceiling with its celestial dreams and constellations. No staring at the bottles of dreams with their beautiful colours and intricate labels. He doesn't pause to examine the ancient *Book of Dreams*, a large, illuminated text that guides dream interpretation and threading. Instead, Jamal skirts around the pedestal on which it sits at the centre of the library and strides to the back. A deep perfume of sandalwood and oud catches me as he passes between the shelves close by. It seems to me he is a man rich in money and pride.

Aunt Moyna shakes her head and takes a deep breath. 'This is sensitive work, Jamal, and it takes time. I am merely one person. My brother and his wife – well, you know . . .'

'Yes, yes.' His voice rises in irritation. 'Their situation is causing me no end of trouble.'

'I did my best to help you with that,' says Aunt Moyna.

Their words make my skin prickle. Aunt Moyna has always been close to me. When my parents betrayed us all she took me in as her own child. I only hope their actions are not adding yet more burdens for my aunt to bear.

Jamal snorts. 'Enough of them. The prince wishes to move forward and look to the future of both our peoples.' Jamal pulls out a red velvet bag from inside his robe. Tied with a golden cord, the bag is bulging with coins.

A big smile yawns across my aunt's face. 'I am sure with such an investment, we would be able to complete the potion by next month,' she says.

'No, next week. The people need certainty. We must bring things to an end sooner than planned.' Jamal strides ahead of my aunt into the depths of the library, with no hint of respect for the dreams it holds.

Click, clack.

Her shoes scatter echoes across the polished wooden floor.

Click, clack.

I stick my head out a little to get a better view. My heart is pounding so hard it's a wonder the entire world doesn't hear me. I see Aunt Moyna at the entrance to the secure section. She puts her hand into her gown and pulls out the intricately wrought library keys. Silver for the library, bronze for our house, and gold for her office, all worn and dulled with age except for one, which she pulls away from the others. It is black as night, with a twisted thread and a head in the shape of a skull. She feeds it in and the lock *clunks*. Then she twists two circular levers and the door creaks open. A bone-chilling torrent of whispers and strangled voices slides out from inside the room. These are the sounds of nightmares and dark dreams, angry at their incarceration and desperate to escape. Destruction by sunlight awaits any nightmares caught in the crossfire when we hunt for dreams, but there seems to be a heavy load of hatred and anger in the room, and it prickles at me like a thousand ants crawling down my back. Aunt Moyna and her visitor step inside. I pull back a little and close my eyes, afraid to breathe, until I hear my aunt pushing the door to the secure section closed, leaving me in a cavernous silence.

I shake myself out of my stupor. Something strange is happening, but working out what it is will have to wait. I need to focus on what I came to do. Tomorrow is reckoning day, when Aunt Moyna adds up the weekly dream scores to root out underperformers who must leave the Citadel and she would use any pretext to eject Rafi. I must find her notebook and reset the score, but as I stretch myself out from behind the sofa I almost trip over.

A pair of eyes is watching me.

CHAPTER THREE

A Strange Invitation

Perched on the top shelf opposite me sits Kala, my aunt's dream creature. He is a common koel, with feathers dark as midnight and blood-red eyes which regard me with cool disdain. He spreads his wings and flaps away with a piercing call.

Coeeee . . .

Coeeee . . .

'Devil bird,' I whisper after him.

Thankfully, the door to the secure section remains closed and his shrieks fail to catch Aunt Moyna's attention.

I crawl out of my hiding place and edge along the wall towards the library entrance and my aunt's office.

It used to be Papa's, but I haven't been inside since he has been gone. Aunt Moyna only calls children in when they have to leave the programme.

The office door is dark oak, solid and thick, with a round brass handle. To my relief the handle twists as I turn it, and I push the door open wide enough to slip into the room. I leave the door ajar so I can hear when my aunt and Jamal leave the secure section.

Beyond the walls of the Citadel, the office looks out over a broad river which passes like a dream, deep and timeless, curling its way to the sea far to the west. On a shelf behind my aunt's large wooden desk is a dream globe that turns through the day and night. It was crafted by our ancestors to find dream creatures in the wild and draw them into the safety of the Citadel. Papa once told me the outer world had become so divided and harsh that the creatures struggled to find dreamers and their population all but melted away, and I can see there are very few spots lit up on the globe right now. I am glad we can hunt dreams through the mirror portals. I wouldn't want to step outside my safe Citadel home when the wider world seems so full of danger.

I dive towards the white coat draped over the back

of Aunt Moyna's chair and fish out her dream ledger. Every hunt receives a score. My aunt keeps it all recorded in her notebook. It means we must work hard for the best dreams. At the end of the year, prizes are given for the top-scoring hunters. Exile beckons for those at the other end of the list.

Securing tonight's grade one dream would have seen Rafi racing up the league but instead he's still festering towards the bottom end. I can't give points for dreams that don't exist – the total must match up with the stock of dreams in the library – but if I transfer some of my points to Rafi, he might get saved from being sent away. I find my name and use Aunt Moyna's pen to carefully deduct the points for a grade two, normally thirty points per thread, from my ledger. Then I flip to Rafi's page, add the points to his tally and replace the book in the pocket, being careful to stow it the same way round.

As I go to switch off the lamp, I notice Lalu perching on a stack of cards on a shelf. I lean over and examine them. Thick pieces of card printed in gold ink and inscribed with extravagant letters which curl and trail like branches. My eyes widen as I read the text.

You are cordially invited to the
First Annual Auction of Dreams –
customized blends to suit all needs!

At 7.30 p.m. on 21 December
in the Library of Forgotten Dreams,
the Citadel of Mirrors

RSVP to Moyna Malou,
Head Librarian.

An auction in the library? Visitors to the Citadel, and judging by the size of the pile of invitations, it will be a large crowd.

I hear the clock in the market square chime eight times. Night is falling.

The sound of voices nips at my ear.

'I am still refining the new potion,' says Aunt Moyna as she leads Jamal towards the office.

I have taken too long.

'The type of threads you need are quite specific,' she says. 'There are few hunters from the old families strong enough to reel them in.'

31

I slide behind the curtain as their voices come closer, eager to understand my aunt's logic. She normally deploys children to hunt dreams because she thinks their young minds are fresh and keen and open, better for finding the rarest of threads. Why does she need the strong minds of older hunters?

My aunt's footsteps pause as they come into the room. 'That's interesting. The door . . .' Her words hang in the air and my heart is squeezed so hard I have to force down a gasp.

'Everything okay?' asks Jamal.

'Everything is just fine.' Aunt Moyna's clickety footsteps circle the room. I am glad the velvet curtains are heavy enough to hide me.

Jamal's voice is louder now as he comes to the window. My forehead starts dripping with sweat. 'We require an advance order for the king, with enough potion to escalate the dose. The whole thing must run like clockwork. Ratnagar is depending on you.'

My hair stands on end. A long time ago, a group of dream threaders left the Citadel and created a factory of dreams in a city far away to the north – Ratnagar. Hidden among the mountains, they forged a bond with Ganipal, Ratnagar's king, to trade dream potions, unhampered by the scrutiny of the Citadel's librarians. They said they wanted to find new customers and be free of the old rules. But as it turned out, what they really wanted was to create nightmares. When the king realized that dark arts and murderous criminals had infested his homeland, he shut down the factory and expelled the dream threaders, breaking all contact with the Citadel and all dream craft, good or bad. Ratnagar sent word to its allies across the north of India urging them to cease trading with us. And so this tiny but powerful kingdom destroyed our reputation, forcing the Citadel to find new markets in lands to the south and even across the sea. In time, the power of dreams to heal and inspire made our people rich once again, but old wounds are not easily forgotten and the story of Ratnagar remains a dark mark in our memories.

Jamal edges close. So close it takes all my will not to sneeze as I catch the scent of his opulent perfume. In my pocket, Lalu has gone very still. I give her a comforting nudge with my little finger.

'Oh, my potion will be fast,' says Aunt Moyna. 'It will be done and gone in a flash, like any well-made dream.'

'Good,' grunts Jamal. 'I will return word to the palace.'

If he is working for King Ganipal, he must know about my parents. In an effort to repair broken bridges, they visited the kingdom two years ago, but when the king refused to restart trading with us again, people say my parents tried to blackmail and poison him and were arrested as traitors and criminals. They are still there, awaiting trial in that foreign land. It seems to me the outer world is a place where power and money turn good people's minds to bad. Perhaps this man Jamal comes here for dreams to reverse whatever poison my parents used to hurt his king.

My aunt pulls her chair away from her desk and opens a drawer. 'Very well. My technician awaits you in the Hall of Mirrors. I'll see you out.'

Jamal pauses as they walk towards the door. 'By the way, I want one of those dream creatures. A magical bird to hunt dreams for me.'

Aunt Moyna laughs. 'These creatures are not pets, Jamal. There were plenty such birds in the outer world, but they have largely died out. All that chaos and conflict are not a good environment for hopes and dreams to flourish. In any case, nice as they are, we don't use them to hunt dreams any more. The hooks and mirrors are far more efficient.'

'When all this is done, perhaps we will make an aviary of such birds,' says Jamal.

My face pales. How can they keep birds in cages, especially such magical creatures as Lalu and Mithi?

'I really must go,' says Aunt Moyna. 'My niece is waiting for me back home.'

She clicks her tongue as Jamal guffaws.

'Didn't see you as the maternal type, Miss Malou.'

'Head Librarian Malou.'

'*Acting* Head.' Jamal laughs.

'Yes, yes, until our plan is complete. And as for my niece, she is but twelve circles of the sun, and will join our efforts in time.'

What efforts? Caging birds and trading secret dream potions?

If Aunt Moyna is trying to help the king of Ratnagar, I wonder why it is all such a big secret.

As they leave the office, my aunt pulls the door closed behind her with a firm thud. A key jangles in the lock and turns and, as their footsteps recede, my blood drains to my feet.

I'm trapped.

CHAPTER FOUR

The Dream Hook of Ibrahim Malou

I pull out my hair clip and slide it into the lock, wiggling it this way and that, just as Rafi taught me, but no amount of rattling will persuade the mechanism inside to budge open.

I poke my head past the curtain and glance out of the window. The library doors groan angrily as Aunt Moyna heaves them open and leads her guest out into the market square, whispering instructions to Jamal as she bids him farewell.

Lalu flutters curiously around above me, casting a flickering blue light into the shadowed corners of the room.

'Careful of the window,' I whisper, 'and the eyes in the skies.'

In the market square, my aunt is almost directly beneath the window as Jamal prepares to leave. Kala rests on her shoulder, shrieking at the horses.

I turn back to Aunt Moyna's desk, and gaze wide-eyed at the bag of gold Jamal brought. I pick up one of the coins and turn it over. It's heavier than it looks and has the figure of a bearded king on one side. He is riding a horse and holds a spear in his hands. My heart skips a beat when I see the word *Ratnagar* inscribed in curly writing. After all the trouble they think my parents created, why would the kingdom of Ratnagar come to the Citadel for aid? Their king outlawed dream trading, yet the size of the pile of gold suggests that Jamal's master has ordered a most precious potion.

The sound of a whip breaks the whirlwind of thoughts in my head, and I slip the coin into my pocket to look at it later.

'Huzzah!' Jamal and his companion spur their horses and set off, cantering to the visitors' gate behind the Hall of Mirrors.

I start pulling at the cabinet doors along the wall with shaking hands, desperate to find somewhere to hide.

The main door to the library swings shut with a thud

and I jump. I'm running out of time when I pull aside a coat hanging on the back of the door. Filled with a rising bile of fear, I rifle through the pockets of my aunt's jacket for another escape route – a key, a pick, something to unlock the door. Anything.

I prick my finger on something sharp and pointy. I close my hand around it and feel the metal hum as I pull it out.

A dream hook.

It is worn with age, though the tip is still sharp enough to reel in a dream. The handle is wooden, inlaid with mother of pearl, and along one side a name has been engraved. I hold it up to the light from the window and gasp.

Ibrahim Malou.

It is my father's name. This is his dream hook. They must have taken it from him when he was jailed.

And then I realize that my way out hangs in front of me.

A full-length mirror within a weathered wooden frame is mounted on the back of the locked door. It's taller than I am and the glass is scuffed. I have heard tell of dream hunters passing through looking-glass portals in the past, of how mirrors are hungry and the glass holds onto fragments of thoughts, so we are taught that the only thing that can safely go through them are dream hooks. And yet . . . what if my aunt has torn up the ancient rules? It would explain how she can come and go throughout the Citadel as if she were a ghost. Perhaps this mirror is the reason she can be anywhere, nowhere and everywhere all at once.

Danger or not, I have no choice and pray my father's hook will respond to me. If it is bound to my kin, the blood link means it should allow me to use it to activate the portal. I wipe a bead of sweat from my forehead as I sweep the hook in a wide circle across the mirrored surface. Without a key I cannot control the destination, and my skin tingles as the looking glass turns smoky. What will I see on the other side? Where will it take me, even if I can pass through?

Click, clack.

The glass turns to liquid as a portal opens.

Click, clack.

Aunt Moyna's footsteps get louder—

I stuff my free hand into my mouth to stop myself from screaming at the mirror.

When it widens enough for me to pass through, my stomach scrunches.

'Lalu, quick!' I hold out my hand, but she nestles into the hair around my shoulder.

Keys jangle outside the locked door—

My feet are stuck, but I have no choice. The glass is a waving mass of liquid and I must go through it. I'll have to return the hook later. I don't think I can pass through without it.

The lock clicks—

I squeeze my eyes and push my face into the glass. Holding my breath, I push further into the mirror. It feels like plunging into a cold bath, but when I emerge I am dry and the mirror behind me sets back into solid glass.

I'm in the entrance to the Hall of Mirrors. Back on the other side the door opens, but just as Aunt Moyna's foot edges into view the vision disappears and all I see is my own messy reflection in the mirror linked to the one in my aunt's office. I pull up my hood and run through the empty hall, heading straight for the doors at the other end. Once I reach the market square I slow down, eyes alert to ravens as I blur into the shadows and cross to the opposite side. I reach the stairs leading to our apartment above the library, tread quickly up them, and breathe a sigh of relief when I can finally shut the door behind me.

I run my hand over my father's dream hook. It connects me to him, and even though I know I shouldn't have taken it part of me tells me it is mine by rights. I hide it with the gold coin under a loose floorboard in my bedroom.

She must never know I was there, and never find what I took.

CHAPTER FIVE

News From Abroad

Moonlight edges through the windows as I wait for my aunt to return. On the kitchen table are newspapers from countries we trade with. My aunt likes to keep up to date with events from the outside world. She says she wants to understand her customers, and this is becoming a widening circle. I flip through some of the papers while having some leftover soup for dinner. I read about a royal palace being built in the kingdom of Bhutari; a baby panda being born in the Forest of Zhang and on the other side of the world the tale of a girl who was lost and then found in the vast rainforest of Amazonia. At the bottom of the pile, my eye is caught by a picture of an old man in a copy of the

Ratnagar Daily News dated 19 December. His profile looks familiar. It's Ganipal, the king of Ratnagar, and my mouth falls open at the story.

KING'S HEALTH CAUSING CONCERN

The Royal Family has gathered at the Palace of Ratnagar as King Ganipal the Third remains under 'medical supervision' amid concerns for his declining health.

The 60-year-old monarch's children and grandchildren have been rushed to the city from around the world as the Council of Elders assemble to discuss the change in His Majesty's condition.

Crown Prince Sakim, who was hunting tigers in Ranthambore, India, was the first to arrive, bringing apothecaries and doctors into Ratnagar to tend to his father.

Concerns over the popular king's health were first raised two years prior, when he suffered an unknown illness that has led to a sad neglect of himself and his kingdom. At the time, two visiting dream threaders from the Library of Forgotten Dreams were found in possession of nightmare potions and arrested for treason. Despite their incarceration, the king has recently suffered further setbacks to his health. Officials are monitoring the activities of dream threaders from the Citadel, with whom all diplomatic and trading ties have been cut.

A statement released by the palace last night reads

as follows: 'Following evaluation, the king's doctors have recommended continued bedrest. He remains comfortable. Prince Sakim will take his father's place as head of state until such time as the king recovers.'

So the king is unwell and, if nothing is done, he may die. He seems to have a kind face. From what I have heard, he is a powerful man, the ruler of a tiny but rich city state who dealt with us fairly until the nightmare trades began. Our diplomatic ties have been cut, so why is Jamal visiting us? Is it so my aunt can help reverse the poison my parents had created?

It is nearly midnight, and I am nestled in my bed when I hear the door open.

Click.

   Clack.

Her footsteps seem slower, less energetic. I wonder if she saw me on the other side of the looking glass. I squeeze my eyes closed when I hear the handle of my bedroom door turn and a low arc of light squeezes in from the outside as my aunt pushes into the room.

'Mimi, are you asleep?' Her voice is hushed. She doesn't sound angry, but I lie still as a mouse. I don't like lying and I can't tell her what I have seen and heard.

Aunt Moyna waits a moment, then closes the door, plunging me back into darkness.

I hear whispers, my name called. I roll over, wondering if she is still by the door, testing me.

Lalu hops away from my pillow and onto my bedside table.

'You look like you're full of nice dreams,' I say. She twitches her head up and down and comes to rest on the edge of my pillow.

I close my eyes, exhausted by the emotions and trials of the day, but as I drift off I hear Lalu squeak. A flash of light floods my closed eyelids and I inch them open to see the dreams inside Lalu shifting from blue to cobalt, to red, and finally to green. The threads slip out of her beak as she shakes her head in pain. They float towards me. Lalu flaps wildly, but my mind sinks into a gloomy, helpless slumber.

*

I am standing on a balcony. Alone. I stand on my tiptoes and pull my eyes above the top of the wall.

My parents are leaving me.

They are walking away from me.

My face is red with rage and confusion, my heart twisting knots on itself.

45

I clutch the brick and try to climb over, my eyes stinging and mouth sore from screaming.

They are going away.

But something is wrong.

My father has discarded his navy-blue silk suit and my mother her yellow sari. Instead, they are dressed in rough cotton jumpsuits.

Prisoners.

A storm is starting overhead, and I shout for them to come home. Get back to shelter before the rain comes and the wind blows.

They can't hear me.

I want to run down the stairs and into the street to follow them. But a pair of hands pulls me back.

'Stay,' says a voice in my head. 'Stop. Be Careful.'

I try to look back, but my head is stuck. Forced to watch them leave me.

'Ma!' I shout. 'You didn't tell me my story.'

She ignores me and keeps walking.

'Papa, what will we have for dinner?'

He stops and turns his head.

My mother too.

I try to scream but I cannot open my mouth.

Their eyes are gone and in their place are hollow pits, dark and shadowed.

Ma lifts her arm to wave goodbye. I hear a groan become a rumble and then a roar. Cracks in the plaster become crevices and the wall behind me falls away. The balcony crumbles and rushes to the ground.

My stomach twists as I fall.

*

I sit up, trying to catch my breath, gripping my wool blanket so tight my fingers hurt.

'Just a nightmare,' I whisper. It has haunted me since my parents left. Is it punishment for something? I know the rest of the Citadel see me as the daughter of traitors; perhaps something deep inside my mind wants to remind me of this.

I wish Lalu would feed me some dream threads so I could forget my parents altogether. Yet tonight she has lost her glow. Her head, tucked into her belly, softly rocks with her breath, but every now and then her tiny body shudders. I stroke her neck and her eyes flick open a moment, then fall back to sleep, exhausted.

There is a tapping at the window and I pull the curtain aside.

'Tala!'

I open the window to him. A red-feathered phoenix, Tala is the first and most constant of the dream creatures. Companion to the head librarian, he left the Citadel when my parents were imprisoned, refusing to bond with my aunt, as if he still waits for my father's return. He comes to visit me, but only when I am alone. I think he is confused about Aunt Moyna, but he has always been kind to me.

I didn't choose my parents.

It isn't my fault.

Tala gives me what I think is a little nod but twitters when he sees Lalu, shivering and weak. He hops through the open window and circles the room. With a soft squawk Tala releases soft dream threads over Lalu, encircling her in a gentle orange glow. As the threads melt into her mind, the golden feathers on Lalu's neck glint and she slowly opens her eyes.

'Thank you!' I whisper, as Tala chirrups a quiet goodbye and sweeps out through the open window and up into the dark of the night, his red feathers soon disappearing into the grey clouds above.

The clock is half in shadow, half in moonlight and tells me it is still five hours till morning. The night breeze chills my shoulders, but my mind is now thrumming.

48

I pull a shawl over myself, creep out of bed to lift the loose floorboard and reach towards my hidden treasure. Though I am ashamed of all they have done, my parents saved me tonight. Papa's dream hook connects me to him and the metal tip sparks as I tighten my hold on it.

A potion to heal a king, an auction of dreams and visitors entering the secure section of the library . . . This is a puzzle bigger than the Citadel itself, and I am going to solve it.

CHAPTER SIX

Trouble in Class

Aunt Moyna has her hands cupped round her breakfast tea, dark as oak and sweet as honey, with puffs of steam spilling over the rim. She takes a careful sip and clears her throat.

'You seem pale, my petal.'

Evidently, she's noticed my lack of sleep.

'I think you are getting emotional, Mimi, and it carries over into your sleep. After yesterday, for example, and that awful boy.'

'He's my friend.'

'Why don't you invite Deena Dilsay over? One of the old families, like us. Her sister works in the—'

'I know, and no. I don't really get on with Deena.'

My aunt gently touches my cheek. 'She's a good student.'

'Rafi isn't so bad. He's one of the few children who doesn't hate me.'

She looks away but she knows what I mean. My parents have tarred me with their treason. I hear the sly whispers and side-eyed glances of my fellow students. Though my aunt is strict, she has always been loyal to me and tries to think of what's best. If only my parents had trusted Aunt Moyna and listened to her advice to help the Citadel grow. Perhaps I can find a way to restore her faith in Rafi by finding dream threads to help her create something really special for King Ganipal. Perhaps that would convince her Rafi is good enough to stay.

'I have some news,' she says. 'The crown prince of Ratnagar has asked me to work with him, perhaps even start joint production of bespoke dream potions. Think about it – the Citadel and Ratnagar, working together once more. The potential for our trade is limitless.'

'I thought the king of Ratnagar cut ties with us after all the trouble with nightmares, and then my parents . . .'

Kala looks at me from his perch on the windowsill and cackles. I hiss at him, and Aunt Moyna rolls her eyes.

'Your parents didn't help,' she says, 'but Prince Sakim is looking to the future. Think of the potential. Ratnagar was once a city rich in trade for us, a staging post for our dealings with the rest of the world while keeping our own Citadel hidden and protected.'

'The king is still in charge there though, isn't he?'

'King Ganipal is succumbing to his illness, and we must be ready to seize the opportunities that may come up when he passes.'

I shudder. 'Do you think he won't get better?'

She looks at me over the top of her teacup. 'Death is something none of us can outrun, my petal.'

'If he dies, what will happen to Ma and Papa?' I ask, my eyes feeling a little stingy.

She ignores the question.

'You're going to help Prince Sakim, to make the king better, aren't you?' I insist.

Aunt Moyna laughs. 'The prince has indeed asked for my help.'

The sky outside the window is like a dull, grey blanket. Winter is closing in and I drape my shawl over my shoulders. Lalu circles around my aunt, flashing shades of silver and blue as the dreams within her squirm and swirl.

'By the twist of her dream threads, your dear little Lalu seems anxious,' says my aunt.

I hold my finger out for Lalu and she flits back to me, gripping so tightly it pinches my skin.

'It's okay,' I whisper, running a finger along the feathers on her back. She flutters her little wings every few seconds but settles as I slip her back into my pocket.

Kala hops from the table onto my aunt's shoulder and caws. His beady red eyes stare at me. If he had eyebrows, I'm pretty sure he would scrunch them. I lift my chin and hold his gaze, then turn away and walk to my room to pack for school. As I take my leave, I remember the gold coin hiding under my floorboards and the red velvet bag it came from. I suppose the king of Ratnagar must be receiving a very fine dream indeed.

*

Madame Griffin has already begun teaching as I creak open the door to the classroom. She is tall and thin, her long grey hair tied back in a ponytail, her face a map of the many years she has taught in the Citadel. My parents were her students before me, and she holds no fear of speaking her mind. Her face is chiselled, almost like a statue, and she directs her proud, majestic gaze to me. Specifically, to my feet.

I follow her eyes and in horror realize I am still wearing my slippers and mismatched bed socks.

'Sorry,' I whisper.

Madame Griffin arches one of her thin eyebrows and turns to the class.

'This morning you will work in pairs, mixing dreams, and we will examine your threads in the dream viewer after lunch.'

On her desk are three jars filled with soft golden-coloured light with sparks of different colours floating through them.

Rafi smiles when he sees me. 'I've been practising, and I think I've worked it out, Mimi,' he says. 'A little jiggle and a wiggle, then a twist and a curl to catch the dream and reel it in.'

'You should have kept the hook hidden in your bag,' I whisper through clenched teeth, pointing at the sharp top of his dream hook peeping out from his trouser pocket for all the world to see.

He nods and with the skill of the street orphan he was before the Citadel, he leans to the side and slides the hook up into his sleeve then down into his bag.

A loud *harrumph* brings my attention to Madame

Griffin, who is staring at us over the top of her thin-rimmed glasses.

'Mimi Malou, could you please remind the class what I just told you all about the activity for today?'

'We are threading . . .' My face flares red.

'Indeed, and what, may I ask, was the warning I gave?' She taps her foot.

I open my mouth, then close it. I'm about to confess that I wasn't listening when the classroom door swings open.

Suri, the dream technician with the streak of white in her hair, appears. She whispers in Madame Griffin's ear then looks across the class with a malicious smile. I feel an ice-cold tingle down my spine as her gaze crosses past me to settle on Rafi.

Madame Griffin shakes her head. 'This is most unheard of,' she says. 'I suggest you wait until we are done with class.' She shoos the assistant away, but our relief is short-lived.

Click, clack.

Madame Griffin scowls.

Click, clack.

A hush falls on the class as Aunt Moyna strides in and squares up to our teacher, though she is a head shorter.

'We have a child in our midst who has no respect for the traditions of goodness and kindness we hold dear in our Citadel,' says my aunt, 'When I arrived in my office this morning I discovered something was missing.' She looks in my direction and my hands go ice cold.

'Really, Moyna, is this necessary?' Madame Griffin's hands are clasped so tightly her fingers are pale.

Aunt Moyna shakes her head sadly. 'I am sorry that Suri and I have had to disturb your lesson this morning,' says Aunt Moyna, 'but trespass and theft are too serious to leave unpunished.'

I scratch the back of my neck. She must know about last night, and I stiffen as she draws close, but she moves past me to Rafi and taps the pointy end of her dream hook on his desk.

'You, boy, are a thief.' Her words are like stones cast into still water. A ripple of dread spreads across the room.

Rafi's mouth falls open and he looks at me with a shadow of fear across his eyes.

'I didn't mean to. I was just practising,' he says.

'Practising thievery. Indeed, you broke into my private office.'

'What? No!' shouts Rafi.

My aunt puts her hands together and closes her eyes a moment as if to calm herself down. It doesn't work. 'You lie,' she says. 'You entered the office and stole my brother's dream hook.'

'That wasn't what I took . . .' Rafi's brow is furrowed.

My face flashes scarlet in anger. 'He didn't steal from you, Aunt Moyna.'

'Oh, look, Suri. Yet again my dear niece is trying to shield this petty thief.'

Aunt Moyna bends down and strokes my hair. I bristle.

'After the mayhem in the Hall of Mirrors, why do you continue your efforts to protect this troublemaker?' She points a finger at Rafi.

'The boy has his faults, Moyna,' says Madame Griffin. 'He may have been a thief before, it is true, but the behaviour I have seen does not reflect what you describe.'

Kala circles the class, shrieking with joy at the chaos unfolding, while Lalu and Mithi huddle in among the other dream creatures in the classroom, alert and watchful.

'Rafi is telling the truth, Aunty. It was me . . .' The

rest of my words fall away as Suri checks his bag and pulls out his hidden dream hook.

Madame Griffin's face falls, and my aunt shoots a dark look at Rafi as she inspects it.

'Ha! Twice a thief, it would seem. Now, where is my brother's hook?' She shakes Rafi's shoulders, her face contorted with rage. 'Where is it?'

I lunge towards my aunt. '*I* have it. *I* took it—' but shouts and scuffles smother my confession as Rafi is hauled, caterwauling, out of his chair.

Aunt Moyna places Rafi's hook in the teacher's pot at the front of the class. Then she and Suri turn to leave.

'Take him to the dream laboratory.'

My hands go clammy as I hear my aunt's parting words.

I run out of the room after them, but my aunt grips my arm.

'Enough of this, Mimi, we will talk later this evening. Return to class.'

'Rafi didn't do anything wrong.' My eyes are burning but I push the tears back. I won't let the others see me cry.

I hear some of them whispering about me as I sit back down.

'He made a mistake being friends with her.'

'Such a precious princess. No one can say anything about *her*.'

Madame Griffin leans close and whispers in my ear. 'Shh. Not now, Mimi. If we want to help, we must do it by stealth.'

CHAPTER SEVEN

The Dream Laboratory

Everything in the Citadel changed when Aunt Moyna took charge. After years of trying to persuade my parents to change things, she acted decisively when she took over to stop the Citadel finally crumbling into poverty and ruin. She brought in more hunters, more shifts and more dreams, but among the newcomers were some who could not or would not hunt as diligently as she demanded, and that was when the dream laboratory came into being. Of the handful of children who have been sent there, none have returned the same and most get sent away shortly after. I doubt even Rafi's fortitude can withstand whatever they actually do in there.

Each day, my nerves become more and more frazzled.

Each day, my feet take me past the tower, but the looks I get from the dream technicians coming in and out send me scurrying away. In class, Madame Griffin's frown gets tighter, to the point where her eyebrows seem to be permanently knitted together, and Aunt Moyna is avoiding me altogether. By the third moonrise I head to the library after school ends with a rescue mission in mind.

The bottles in the library are grouped by character and emotion, ready for the dream threaders to mix the components they need for their potions. Dreams of happiness and curiosity used to form the largest part of the library stock, but in recent months we have been told to hunt a mix of other feelings and emotions. Purple for pride, silver for success, blue for bravery, and sometimes even red for anger.

My favourite section is where the dreams of childhood memories are stored. Yellow and golden tinted dream threads swirl for my attention, throwing playful sparks and glinting as the sunlight falls on them through the windows, protected from melting away by the enchanted glass they are contained in.

I pull a ladder towards me when I reach the aisle and climb up to fetch the bottle I am after. I put my hand to the glass and remember the summer night last year when we found the dream it holds. Inside is a grade one happiness dream so powerful it scattered rainbows and starlight even as we bottled it. The librarian supervising the hunt that night told me it would be used in dream potions for years to come, that only fragments would be needed to create sequences that could heal physical as well as mental ailments, but despite that the bottle has sat unused, gathering dust.

'Come, Lalu.' I hold out my finger and she hops onto the tip as we prepare to do a little thievery of our own.

I am not allowed to check out dreams yet – only certified dream threaders are permitted to do that. I look around to make sure the coast is clear, then uncork the bottle and let Lalu perch on the rim. She dips her beak into the open neck, her body glowing bright golden yellow as she catches a tiny thread in her beak.

Voices approach from the other side of the shelf so I reseal the bottle and tuck Lalu in my pocket. Then I hastily push the bottle behind another just as a librarian arrives. It is the lady who checked me in on our last dream hunt. I quickly wrap a scarf around my shoulders to hide Lalu's glow.

'*Brrrr*. It is getting cold, isn't it!' I rub my arms and give a fake shiver.

She looks at me, eyebrows furrowed. 'What are you doing in here at this time of day?' Her voice is low, and she glances towards the other side of the library.

'Just researching,' I say.

She shakes her head and shoos me away from the shelves. 'Get along with you now. The technicians are in here tonight, so we're clearing people out early.'

'Yes, I should go. Wouldn't want to bump into Suri,' I whisper.

'No, you wouldn't.' The librarian smiles.

I let her lead me towards the entrance and bid goodbye. 'May your thoughts be luminous, Madame.'

The librarian taps her head politely. 'May your dreams shine ever brightly, Miss Malou.'

She turns away and pushes her trolley back towards the office, where her dream creature, an ancient barn owl, is dozing above the doorway.

I slip out and mingle with the crowds in the market square, where people are beginning to scatter like ants to their homes in the residential side of the Citadel, but I peel off when I pass a rough, circular tower set in the outer wall of the fortress. The wide oak door

63

of the dream laboratory is bolted shut and I knock softly.

Nothing.

If the dream technicians are in the library, there might be a chance someone nicer is on the door of the laboratory. I knock again and again, until a key rattles in the lock and a pair of spindly hands pull the door open. I gasp when I see the face.

'Maya!' I say. 'You look . . .' I'm about to say 'different' and stop myself.

I used to hunt with Maya Dilsay, Deena's older sister. She was a gifted student who unfortunately did so well in school she was shepherded early into the technician training pathway, losing her smile and her kindness in the process.

'You.' Maya seems to have aged a decade. With her hair pulled back and her eyes half closed, she looks me up and down, and I shiver at how much she now resembles her less gentle sibling. 'What do you want? I doubt your aunt would send her precious niece here.'

'My friend Rafi,' I whisper, 'he's been sent here.'

'So?' She suppresses a thin smile.

'I just want to check he's okay.'

'You can't,' she hisses back at me.

'Please, can I just talk to him?'

'He's sleeping. He'll come out once they have finished work on him.'

Her words bring a sharp stinging to my eyes. I blink away my tears and push on the door. A flicker of guilt seems to cross Maya's mind and she looks down, slowly shaking her head.

'I'm sorry, Mimi. I can't let you in.' She clasps my hand gently and moves it away, pushing the door closed.

I retreat to a shadowed corner where the tower meets the wall and peer up through soft sprinkles of rain. A harsh electric light spills out from the windows above. I start feeling for cracks and gaps in the brickwork. Then, using a drainpipe to steady my ascent, I pull myself up by pushing my feet into the spaces and onto the ledges, easing myself upwards, holding onto the black iron drainpipe as I reach higher and higher.

The breeze ruffles my hair, but I pull my hood close to protect Lalu. I don't want anyone on the ground to spot the luminous dreams she is carrying. When I reach the first floor, I stretch myself out towards the closest window. With my outstretched hand I grab hold of the frame, straining hard as I pull across and grab a foothold on the window ledge. My arms ache, but I hold my breath as I hear voices drifting out from inside the tower.

'He's not an easy one to crack,' says a woman's voice. I edge my eyes past the brickwork. She is facing away from me and talking to her colleague. They wear the khaki green uniform of the Citadel guards.

'It doesn't matter. The boss wants to calm the boy down. She might use his dreams for the Ratnagar job. Says he's got a good bit of bite in him,' says a man sitting at a desk on the other side of the room. His face is half lit by a bronze table lamp that sends a cone of light across the desk. He has thick glasses and the kind of moustache that must take hours to tame each morning, twisted and pointed into two arrowheads under his long, pointy nose.

I freeze as a dream creature flies across the room and lands close to the window. The raven sits at the windowsill and caws. Instinctively I pull back, but a loose stone comes away from the brickwork and falls onto the sill with a thud. I hang onto the drainpipe and sink into the shadows where the tower meets the wall. The window groans as it is jerked open and the female guard's head pops out, looking down at the market square below. I grip onto the bracket round the drainpipe with every bit of strength I can summon. If the woman looked to her right, she would see me, but she pulls her head back in.

'Did you hear that?' she says.

'Some kid throwing stones,' says the man. 'Shut the window. I'm cold.'

I take a deep breath before hoisting myself further up the tower. The next floor has a window just above and, when I reach it, my arms and legs are shaking with exhaustion.

This time the room is silent. There is a flickering electric light hanging in the centre of the room. Below it are three beds in a line, all made up with sheets and pillows, all empty, except for one.

'Rafi,' I whisper as I put a hand to the window. His eyes are squeezed shut and it would seem there is at least one dream technician who isn't in the library tonight. Suri leans over him, her back to the window. Rafi's face grimaces as she holds her dream hook over the gap between his eyes. As she twists the hook, a tangle of dream threads is drawn from his mind. They coil and fight to work themselves back into Rafi, but her hook is too powerful, and she lifts them away with ghastly precision. One by one she drops her catch into a line of waiting bottles. They form a sorrowful spectrum as the bright, happy dream threads in the first few bottles change to thoughtful blues, the dark purple of despair, and angry reds fighting to escape from their confines. In the corner of the room a dark metal birdcage sits on a wooden dresser and inside it sits Mithi, forlorn, fluttering up and down every now and then before realizing there is no point. Suri's dream creature, Carab, sits on the top of the cage, shrieking caws at the trapped chiffchaff. I cling on, watching in cold fury as Suri seals the final bottle and leaves the room.

Without a moment's hesitation I tug at the window to ease it open, but it jams and won't lift any more than a small sliver of a gap, the gap too small for me to pass through. But it is not too small for a hummingbird. I ease back my scarf and release Lalu out from her hiding spot.

'Help Rafi,' I plead. She looks at me and nods. Then, in a luminous blur, my hummingbird dream creature is gone. She zips through the gap under the window and nestles next to Rafi. Hidden from view, she nuzzles into his neck and opens her beak. A strand of the dream she carries fizzes a little and sparks into a soft rainbow, melting into his skin. As Lalu flees back to me, Rafi opens his eyes and turns his head and I realize this is not the Rafi I know. Outwardly he's the same person – about my age but more golden brown than me, with scruffy brown hair and a gap between his two front teeth – but his smile is hollow and behind his eyes lurks a shadow of fear.

Rafi starts to sit up. I raise my hand then put my finger to my mouth.

He slowly looks around the room then, realizing he is alone. He shuffles to the window.

'What did they do?' I ask.

Rafi shakes his head. 'I can't remember. It was like falling into darkness, all my dreams floating out of my head.' He rubs his eyes.

'I'm so sorry.' He is here because of me. Blamed for a theft he did not commit.

'You didn't do all this,' he says. 'Anyway, you came, didn't you?' He clears his throat. 'You pulled me out of that darkness. I saw a flash of orange light and felt a rush of happiness. I saw my old home, my friends in Mumbai, my mother before she died. That was you. You saved me with a dream, didn't you?'

I look behind Rafi to the door and nod. 'Let's talk later. I'll keep coming back till they let you go.'

'They said I can go home tomorrow. They wanted to clear my mind of dreams, to make me a better hunter.' His eyes darken as he looks at the row of bottled dream threads arranged at the end of the bed. 'And now they have.'

Extracting dreams by force is something that was only ever done by Citadel doctors to treat people with repeated nightmares, but Aunt Moyna seems to be using it as punishment. Perhaps she thinks it will clear rebellious thoughts from difficult minds, but a darker motive occurs to me. Could she be using these fresh, forcibly extracted dreams for evermore powerful potions?

Whatever my aunt's reasoning, even if it is to help the ailing king of Ratnagar, the idea of taking dreams from the minds of children against their will makes my insides churn and my stomach burn. I hide my anger from my friend.

'Be strong, Rafi. Stay calm and try not to act like . . . well, like your normal self, I guess. Say nothing and I'll see you tomorrow.'

'Okay, Mimi. I'll pretend my mind is blank, just how they like it.' He nods his head. 'To luminous thoughts.'

'And shining dreams.' Lalu settles on my shoulder as I whisper my farewell and inch back down to the ground.

CHAPTER EIGHT

Dangerous Visions

I breathe a sigh of relief when I see Rafi waiting for me outside school the next morning. He seems to have a spring back in his step, but when we reach class his face drops as our fellow students fall silent. A few murmur a greeting to him, but most look away. He's not the only orphan here from the outer world, but all of them want to fit in, so there is no chance of camaraderie among children fighting for their own future.

Madame Griffin, in contrast, puts on a rare but brief display of warmth and places her hand on Rafi's shoulder as he sits at his desk.

'We'll try dream-mixing again today,' she says. 'I imagine you'll be good at this, Rafi.'

Rafi doesn't let things get to him for too long, so with a big smile he holds out his dream-mixing bowl for Madame Griffin to drop snippets of dream threads into it.

We use our dream hooks and tweezers to transfer the threads into our mixing jars. The first thread from my share slips over the edge of the bowl like a silvery eel. Wiggling, draping, and coiling as it jumps into the jar and collects in a jumbled loop at the base. I hold my breath and add the second dream. This one glows orange and seems more excitable as it rushes into the jar to meet the first thread. I grin as I watch the two dream threads react to each other. Their ends curl upwards, then intertwine like a rope, curling around each other. I try to coax the final thread in the mixing bowl onto my hook. It is not as luminescent and, as I lift it up, it hangs limp. This must be a forgettable dream, but Madame Griffin is always telling us every dream has value. It sits at the lip of the mixing jar, half hanging over the edge. At one point it starts to slip onto the table, and I rush to catch it. As I push it in, it catches the edge of my fingertip, sending a spark up my hand. I catch the scent of sandalwood and oud. A scarlet cloak flashes across my mind and I wipe my forehead, trying to forget. I push the dream towards the other threads, where it is embraced into a helical thread.

'You have five minutes remaining,' says Madame Griffin. At the front of the class, she demonstrates the threading technique to a couple of new children. They gasp as she twizzles and twists the multi-coloured loop into a tight ball. With a tiny hint of a smile, she lets the children shake the bottle gently. They cackle and shriek with amazement as it bounces against the glass, fizzing and sparking.

When we've all settled down, Madame Griffin taps her desk to move us on to viewing the contents of our work.

'Everybody, time to read some dreams.'

We file into a dimly lit room, where each table has a wooden box intricately carved with dream imagery across the lid. These are high-magnitude dream viewers. Instead of just showing a dream thread, they can show the story within. The looking glass nestled in the box is about as small as my hand. As it senses the dreams close by, the reflective surface flickers and shimmers.

Rafi and I join the children clustered around Madame Griffin as she demonstrates how to read a thread, and we clap with delight as we watch her dream story unfold.

The looking glass throws up a vision of a range of snow-capped mountain peaks. Fresh snow crunches underfoot and, at a cave arched into the mountainside, the dreamer puts their hand in their pocket and pulls out a jade dragon figurine; they place it on the ground and, as they do so, the jade melts away, revealing a tiny, living dragon. It flaps its wings. As it flies, it grows, swooping in ever-growing circles until it is soaring up to the tops of the mountains and back, a majestic beast with a brilliant, golden twinkle in its eyes. I feel a lump in my throat, wondering how pale my dream will look in comparison. The dragon rises into the sky, soaring across a blue sheet of sky and up towards the moon. Then the dream breaks off and astonished silence is broken by loud applause.

Madame Griffin makes her way around the class, with encouraging nods and occasional raises of her famous eyebrows, arriving at our desk with an expectant air and lips struggling to hold back an encouraging smile.

Mithi and Lalu sit on the desk in front of us as she puts Rafi's dream thread into the viewing box first. She drops the dream onto the viewer and my mind is lifted as we watch children playing on a sun-splashed golden beach where waves slap down in a slow rhythmic beat, like a song of the sea.

'That's beautiful,' I whisper to him.

'I think it reminds me of home,' he says, 'but I am starting to forget what home looked like.'

My throat tightens. As much as I need Rafi's friendship in the Citadel, I know he might be safer in Mumbai, whatever the hardships. I might not be able to save him next time.

Madame Griffin gives me a hopeful nod. 'Mimi, let's see what you have crafted.'

I guide the dream onto the looking glass of my dream viewer with a fluttering mix of hope and foreboding. The third thread in my potion seemed most uninspired. At best I hope the dream will be a little happy, at worst forgettable. As my dream melts into the mirror, the reflective surface softens into a rippling liquid and then, as it clears, the dream sequence unfolds . . . and I realize the outcome, far from being happy or even forgettable, is far worse. Inside the dream is a vision of books and rows of bottles, and a yellow sofa with the evening sun setting through the windows of the Library of Forgotten Dreams. Bile rises in my chest as a flash of scarlet cloak enters the viewing screen and Lalu hops onto an outstretched hand. My hand.

I am in the dream.

I pull the dream viewer to my chest and look up, but there is no hiding it now. My memories are imprinted into the thread and now they are on the screen. Memories that show a forbidden scene which could be highly incriminating. Madame Griffin turns to the other children and signals the end of class. Raising a hand to me, she takes the dream viewer, and she and I watch the dream play on a little. My stomach twists over itself. There I am walking through the library. There I am again, spying on my aunt and the strange visitor from Ratnagar.

Madame Griffin tuts and shakes my dream reader, letting the image fizzle away. 'You touched the thread, Mimi, and it drew in your own thoughts.'

I shuffle my feet and nod.

She lowers her voice and glances at the door. 'What were you thinking, going to the library after hours?'

'I was worried about Rafi after our mirror broke during a hunt. So I went to the library to see if I could do something to help him.' I bite my lip and decide I won't tell her about changing Rafi's score in my aunt's ledger.

'A troublesome situation,' concludes Madame Griffin, snapping her book shut. She flicks her eye at the door again.

'Slippery fingers can betray our thoughts. A dangerous combination.' She nods and stands up, lifting her bag over her shoulder, and we leave the classroom together.

We walk in silence as we pass through the near-empty school playground. Then she leans in close. 'Be very careful, Mimi.'

'I will, Madame, but I want to make sure Rafi is safe too.'

Madame Griffin's voice now falls to a whisper. 'What happens to Rafi next depends on his behaviour. You need to stay in line and stop taking responsibility for his failures. Help him, yes, but do not test your aunt's loyalty.'

I have never questioned Aunt Moyna's feelings before, but Madame Griffin's words leave a chill running down the back of my neck. My aunt is becoming a stranger and my own place in the Citadel feels more and more unclear.

Something has to change, but who will help me?

CHAPTER NINE

Learning to Hide

On Friday, I have to suffer sitting beside Deena Dilsay in history class. She has never forgiven me for being the first to get a dream creature. She and her best friends Lili Beg and Jamu Dola have an inflated sense of their own importance. Like me, they are all descended from some of the original dream threaders in the Citadel. Unlike me, they think they are better than the newcomers.

'Oh, hi, Mimi,' Deena drawls. 'Dream threading was interesting yesterday. Mine turned out well, did you hear?'

'Lucky you.' My voice is flat, my fists curled tight.

Jamu is sitting in front of us. He turns around and

smirks at me. 'What happened to your dream again?' The corner of his mouth curls ever so slightly upwards. 'Oh yes. First rule of dream threads: never touch the dream thread.'

'It was a mistake,' I whisper.

'Oh, sure,' says Deena. 'Must have been super awkward though, no?' Her dream creature, a vomit-green parrot called Sniffle, lets out a sharp cackle.

'Feel free to focus on your own issues, Deena. I heard last time we did dream threading you turned a baby's dream into a deeply frightening nightmare.' I force a tight smile at her. 'You do know we're a library of dreams, not a factory of nightmares?'

Deena tuts but I pull out my history notebook and studiously avoid her gaze.

At the front of class our teacher, Monsieur Julin, comes in pushing an old freestanding mirror on wheels before him and turns it to face us. He wears a cloth cap and round spectacles and has a thicket of a beard that hides his expression so well I never know if he's pleased or annoyed.

Rafi leans across from his desk. 'That mirror looks properly ancient.'

He almost looks back to normal but he seems to

have lost a little sparkle from his eyes. The laboratory has tamed him, it would seem.

'Mimi, why don't you come and try your dream hook on the mirror?' says Monsieur Julin. 'After all, it was your ancestor who laid the first stones of the Citadel.'

'Teacher's pet,' hisses Deena.

'Citadel snake,' I whisper back.

Deena arches a brow at me. 'At least my parents aren't traitors.'

Her words make my eyes sting and I look away as I join Monsieur Julin at the front of the class.

The glass in the mirror is tinted with shades of grey and yellow, and along the frame are a series of carvings I recognize as alchemy symbols. Monsieur Julin hands me my dream hook and I run a circle across the glass. It turns to shimmering liquid, opening a portal that looks over a wall of silver-barked kulu trees.

'Ghost trees,' whispers Rafi.

'Correct!' says Monsieur Julin. 'The Forest of Garh surrounds our Citadel, and though many may wander close to our walls, they will not enter uninvited. Do we know why?' He peers at Jamu over the top of his glasses.

'Because it's so boring here,' says Jamu.

The class sniggers. Monsieur Julin pulls his glasses up and narrows his eyes slightly, but, on the whole, a man with a beard looks the same whether he is angry or not.

'This –' his voice has a tetchy undertone as he points to the trees on the other side of the mirror – 'is a Citadel in hiding. A spell was cast to protect our ancestors.'

The story of the Citadel begins with persecution. Three hundred years ago, a small band of alchemists hunted forgotten dreams, creating mirrors and hooks to find and capture those delicate night thoughts. Their potions brought them wealth and fame, but as word of their power spread to the royal court it sparked a backlash of fear and jealousy. The king of Mariashtra, Shivajun the Second, sent the dream hunters into exile, forcing them to create a new, hidden homeland.

Monsieur Julin clears his throat. 'In our next lesson, we will be learning about the spell of protection and how it keeps us safe,' he says, 'which means we will take a trip into the forest.'

A fountain of hollers and hoots erupts at the promise of a school trip.

Far away from the outer world, tucked on a hill in

the dense Forest of Garh, the Citadel is protected by a powerful spell which renders it invisible to the naked eye. The only entrance is the main gate, which becomes visible when it is opened at dawn but is hidden behind the spell when closed at dusk. Dream trade has brought prosperity to the Citadel, but painful memories of kings and emperors run deep.

I think about Jamal visiting on behalf of Prince Sakim and remember that today is 21 December. Tonight will be the auction of dreams. I wonder if Monsieur Julin knows about these secretive visits well after trading hours, but the bell for lunchtime rings, interrupting my thoughts. I race out, driven towards the dining hall by hunger so tightly knotted in my stomach that I am not put off by the slop landing on my plate – a scoop of rice and some murky curry over it.

Rafi spots me and pulls up his chair.

'There's talk of strange people seen coming into the Citadel. More than the normal comings and goings.'

I swallow a chewy mouthful of food and push my plate away. 'So? All kinds of traders come and go. It's how we make our money.'

Rafi leans in close. 'They say people are even coming in from Ratnagar.'

I cast a glance sideways. Deena, Lili and Jamu are seated at the next table with their giggling friends.

'The king of Ratnagar is unwell,' I whisper. 'Perhaps he needs a dream potion. Where else would they go for that?'

Rafi raises his eyebrows. 'So you think they are coming here to buy potions they banned over there?'

'He's the king – I suppose they'd try everything,' I say.

Rafi points to my food. 'You going to finish that?'

I push over my plate and he scoops up some rice and a piece of chicken, wolfing it down. 'If the king of Ratnagar is close to death, I wonder if your aunt is trying to patch things up with the rest of the royal family . . . you know, after your parents and all that . . .'

We sit silently for a minute. 'Maybe, but there seem to be a lot of secrets in the library,' I say. 'They need unfolding.'

For now it's information and not dreams we need to gather.

CHAPTER TEN

The First Annual Auction of Dreams

At a table in the library entrance Aunt Moyna sits, with her staff arranged around her like sheep, watching, brooding, taking instruction. She smiles but it turns sour when she sees Rafi following me in.

'What are you two doing here?'

'We're just studying for a dream-threading test,' he says.

'Okay.' My aunt taps at her watch. 'But the library will close shortly. Special event on tonight.'

As the other librarians scatter, I notice Suri, who gives us a slippery smile as she lets herself past the reception desk and takes a seat next to my aunt.

When we reach my yellow sofa, Rafi grabs a book

and sits down, leaning back into the soft cushions, but I pull his sleeve.

'We don't have time for bedtime stories.'

He follows me behind the sofa, where we scrunch ourselves into a shadowed corner.

'We need to hide till after they close, so we must make ourselves as small and as quiet as we can,' I say. 'Hard for you, I know.'

He does an imaginary zipper across his mouth, but he can't contain himself for long. 'My legs are aching. Can't we hide somewhere else?'

I shake my head fiercely and in whispered snatches tell Rafi more about the king, about Jamal's visit and the invitations to the auction I saw in my aunt's office. We crouch behind the sofa, our dream creatures tucked into our arms. We stay hidden, keeping still as stone for so long that pinpricks skitter along my feet and toes. I shuffle a little but freeze as we hear people leaving the library.

'I didn't see Mimi leave,' says my aunt to one of the technicians. 'She and that boy must have slipped out. Check the upper gallery just in case.'

Then the lights dim and the library doors swing shut. I'm suddenly filled with a heavy realization at how dangerous my plan is.

From behind the sofa, Rafi and I watch as Aunt Moyna opens the door to the secure section, letting the lock fall to the ground with a clunking, metallic thud. Rafi's mouth falls open when we hear the whispers and threats of the dark nightmares within as they seek minds to infect and sleepers to poison.

'Why is she storing those nightmares?' whispers Rafi.

'I don't know. She must be so busy with the dream potion for the king.'

'Maybe the auction is so she can sell dreams to other places too?' suggests Rafi.

I shrug. I can't second-guess my aunt, but I am sure she wants the best for the Citadel, even if she isn't the gentlest of souls.

The main library doors swing open again with a groan, and my aunt strides to the entrance. A myriad of footsteps and a sea of strange voices from across the outer world enter our sacred space. Laughing, tittering, gossiping, their unfamiliar words float around the room, turning the familiar to unfamiliar. The gates into the Citadel must have been busy tonight.

I peek out over the back of the sofa and spy figures dressed in an array of clothes. I see gilded turbans, dark bearskin hats, smartly tailored dinner jackets and frilly, flowing ballgowns. I'm struck by a woman whose skin is white as snow and is clad in a fine silk gown, a fox fur draped around her shoulder. She has sparkly blue eyes and is in animated conversation with Jamal, the envoy from Ratnagar.

'My friends –' My aunt lifts her arms as she addresses her guests, her voice strong and confident. 'Welcome to the Library of Forgotten Dreams.'

The voices in the audience fall to mumbles; there are clinks of glassware as drinks and snacks are circulated.

'My dream technicians will bring you a list of the potions on offer,' continues my aunt. 'I am sure you will agree they offer excellent value for money. Bidding begins in ten minutes.'

A fizz of anticipation bubbles up from the crowd as they murmur in appreciation, clinking their glasses.

'Tonight,' says my aunt, 'we are proud to offer dark dreams. Pure, powerful and perfectly perilous.'

A shadow crosses above my head.

'Kala,' I whisper, without looking at Rafi, and we lean back.

My aunt's dream creature caws and lands close by, poking his head over the back of the sofa. Rafi and I hold our breath, waiting for the koel to grow bored with us, but he looks down into the darkness and sweeps his gaze around. Then he looks back up and squawks.

Coeeee!

He shrieks and shrieks again and again, demanding the attention of my aunt.

Coeeee!

Eventually Aunt Moyna pauses and someone coughs in the awkward silence.

'Go check on Kala, will you?' she says.

I clench my jaw, staring back at the bird with determined eyes. I try willing him away, but he cackles and caws.

Heavy footsteps come to a halt on the other side of our hiding place. A bead of sweat trickles down the back of my neck.

'He seems agitated.' A woman's voice.

The footsteps come closer still. All I can hear now is the pounding rhythm of my heart. I clutch Rafi's hand. Lalu and Mithi quiver their wings between us.

Click, clack.

'What is going on?' My aunt's voice is dangerously close, and so high and tinkly I know she must be furious about the interruption.

Kala hops down behind the sofa and pecks my ankle.

I close my eyes tight, waiting for the inevitable.

'He's behind the sofa,' says Suri.

I stare into Kala's evil red eyes, holding my breath and Rafi's hand. He is shaking.

'Who?' says my aunt.

Kala opens his beak and shrieks. My heart is thundering as he hops up onto the back of the sofa again and turns his head towards Aunt Moyna.

'Kala, madam,' says Suri. 'He was behind the sofa.'

'What of it?' says my aunt sharply. 'Let him be. We must get back to business.'

The dream threads in Kala glow a dangerous mix of green and red. Realizing he has been ignored he shoots up like a spear, racing towards the lofty ceiling.

Rafi opens his scrunched eyes. We both know how close to being found we came.

'My apologies for the interruption,' says my aunt. 'So, let's begin. For generations, the librarians have provided customized dreams for young and old around the globe, but I have come to realize there is so much more we could do. We should be offering a wider variety of potions and broadening our clientele.'

'Hear, hear,' says a gruff voice. I recognize the speaker as Jamal.

'For centuries we have catered to the needs of everyday folk,' my aunt continues, 'threading dreams for them to sleep, to learn, to love, to heal their illnesses.'

I think of the ancestors who built the Citadel, stone by stone, on the income from this trade.

'We are going to change this. Let everyday folk find their own dreams in future . . .'

Aunt Moyna pauses a moment and light applause ripples across the crowd.

'Our collection of dreams available tonight offers raw, unbridled power to our paying customers. Potions with which anything is possible!' She lets out a tinkly laugh and the audience is thunderous in its applause.

'What is she talking about?' asks Rafi. 'Dream potions can't offer power, can they? Unless . . .'

I squeeze Rafi's arm as the realization hits me.

'Unless she's selling nightmares!'

CHAPTER ELEVEN

Three Drops for Murder

I put a finger to my lips, and we crouch lower, listening in horror as my aunt feeds fearful ideas to a hungry crowd.

'From tonight, the Library becomes a place of strength, discipline and respect, not a storage room for childhood dreams. So let us begin with Lot One. A potion to inspire fear in your enemy. Not quite enough to kill, but near enough.'

Ice runs through my veins. All I want is for the Citadel to be a place of peace and happiness, but here is Aunt Moyna changing my community out of all recognition. My thoughts lose their sense of direction, but Rafi puts his hand on my shoulder and my mind spins back to the auction unfolding in the library, to the voices of the bidders and the sums of money rising higher and higher.

On a table behind my aunt are a number of old green bottles, all packed with hissing nightmares. The dream technician stands beside them, her eyes scanning the crowd. As she turns her head in our direction a cold shiver runs down the back of my neck. I pull further into the shadow, hidden from the crowd by the sofa and several rows of dream-stacked shelves.

'Let's check out the secure section at the back,' says Rafi. 'Can we get there without being seen? Perhaps we can get some evidence, maybe even do a bit of sabotage?'

I puff out my cheeks. 'Okay, let's try, while everyone is focused on my aunt and the bidding.' I point to a service ladder behind us. It leads to the upper galleries where the lights are out. 'We can use that route to move from here across to the back of the library. There's another ladder that goes back down near the secure section.'

We take off our shoes and I send Rafi up the ladder first. As he gets on the first rung the metal creaks a little and we pause. A screech from above suggests Kala is still watching, but my aunt is taking bids and his call goes unnoticed. The bidding for the first lot has ended, and in the applause that follows I join Rafi in the gallery, where we retreat into a cubicle and wait.

There is silence for a moment and through the arched railing on the upper level I see Suri casting her eyes across the library. For a moment, she pauses her gaze on Kala, who has given up cawing and is sitting on a shelf behind us. I clench my fist ready to fight, but suddenly my aunt is instructing Suri to bring out the next lot and her attention moves on.

'Lot Two,' says my aunt. She holds up a bottle in the form of a harpy. Half bird, half human. 'A potion to strike fear of separation. A small dose once a day will inspire the recipient to be grateful for your protection.'

The colour in the bottle tweaks a memory. Blue, red and black . . . It makes me catch my breath. Rafi pokes me, then points to the back of the library.

'Come on! We don't know how many lots there are.'

The bidding below comes thick and fast as we creep from aisle to aisle, keeping ourselves hidden as best we can until we reach the final ladder.

'Are you ready for this?' I ask.

Rafi nods and one after the other we scamper down to the lower level, close to the secure section. The black key hangs from the lock and the door to the storage room sits slightly ajar. Together we cross the threshold.

Inside, the small, windowless room is lit with a dirty, evil glow by row upon row of bottles filled with dark dreams and nightmares. Although they are bottled, these threads are so powerful their sound seeps through the glass and into our minds. I shiver as their threats wrap themselves around us. Taunting, teasing, terrifying.

'How can there be so many?' says Rafi.

'She must have stopped the destruction process ages ago,' I say. Normally when we find nightmares on the dream hunt, we bottle them for destruction by sunlight.

The creak of floorboards outside stops my heart a moment. Someone is close by.

Rafi and I push ourselves into a gap behind one of the shelves, our eyes squeezed closed and fingers in our ears to block out the fear and hatred spilling out of the bottles in the room. We cup our dream creatures in our hands, to stop the glow of their dreams from catching anyone's attention.

From the corner of my eye, I spot Aunt Moyna. She is pulling bottles off shelves, looking for something specific.

'Ah,' she says when she finds it, and she hurries off,

pushing the door closed. I hold my breath, hoping she doesn't lock it, but thankfully she's in too much of a rush as we hear her begin the next auction lot.

As I stretch out of our hiding spot, I notice a small bottle on the shelf next to me. I glance at the label, and it's as if a shard of ice has shot through me:

> *Solution of Nightmares for Mimi Malou.*
> *1 drop for fear. 2 drops for terror.*

I touch the bottle and feel a jolt. It's the nightmare I have been having in my sleep on and off for the past two years . . .

The balcony . . . My parents lost in the crowd . . .

Alone. I am alone . . .

I feel a rise of bile in my chest. Aunt Moyna – she has been poisoning me with nightmares! But why? With a shaky hand I pick up the bottle. The vicious dream threads hurl themselves at the glass as they sense my presence and I drop it quickly into my bag.

My emotions swarm like angry wasps, desperate to fight back. I want to smash every bottle in this pestilent room, but I clench my fists and simmer and sweat, knowing I am just a breath away from my aunt outside.

95

'Look!' says Rafi. He points to a dusty grey bottle, ornately crafted with a gold cap moulded into the shape of a crown. We peer at the price tag tied round the neck: fifty pieces of gold per thread.

'Whew,' I say, 'this lot must be worth a fortune!' Then I gasp as I read the label stuck on the bottle:

> *Custom blend for King Ganipal of Ratnagar.*
> *Freshly crafted nightmares.*

Rafi picks up the bottle and nearly drops it as the threads inside explode into life, jumping against the stopper so violently it starts to rattle as the nightmares seek a way to escape and infect him. His face is pale as he puts the bottle down and whispers the dose instructions.

'"One drop to frighten. Two drops to terrify. Three drops for murder." Oh, Mimi!'

We stare at the bottle and then at each other and my chest goes so tight I can barely dare take a breath. I thought she was being paid to cure the king of Ratnagar, but this would kill him! *Does Prince Sakim know about this?* I think. *Could it be from before my aunt's time?* Then another thought strikes me: *Perhaps it's part of my parents' treachery.*

96

But that cannot be true. I've been having the nightmares since living with my aunt. If she's been slipping those to me, perhaps she has been creating harmful potions for the king of Ratnagar too. I wonder who else is caught up in this web of lies and poison.

We hear a cough from the other side of the door. A shadow darkens the light filtering into the room.

Rafi tugs my sleeve. 'Come on. We should go.'

Hidden by the shelves, we sneak a look out into the main library. Suri is standing by the door, keeping guard. Neither of us can barely breathe for fear of being heard, but then the crowd breaks out into loud applause and my aunt announces the end of the sale.

As Suri leaves to help the guests gather their things, Rafi and I pull up our hoods, ready to slip through to the back door of the library, but when I grab the handle, it won't budge. I rattle it as gently as I can, my hand all sweaty, but it holds firm.

'Wait,' I say as Rafi shifts nervously, looking for a hiding place.

I take out my hairgrip and carefully fiddle with the lock. It *clunks* angrily as the mechanism gives way but before we can open the door and slip out my aunt's voice comes flying this way.

'Suri, did you hear something? Check what that noise was.'

I hold my breath, too scared to push the door open as Suri's footsteps draw close. If we open the door now, she will see us, so we scramble under the nearest table.

I feel a peck on my toes and look down into two red, beady eyes.

I bite my lip as Kala turns his head a little one way then another, as if deciding whether to bother trying to raise the alarm on us again. I find a small piece of bread in my pocket and toss a bird-sized morsel to him.

He bends forward and examines it, then picks it up and lifts his head, swallowing the piece in one go.

'Hello?' calls Suri. 'Anyone there?'

The floorboards creak and my heart thumps so loudly I am sure she will hear it and find us.

From between the shelves comes a flying screech as Kala whizzes past the technician and out into the main section of the library.

'Ugh. Stupid bird,' mutters Suri.

We sigh with relief as she turns back, and use the distraction to slip out into the night.

In my pocket is the bottle of nightmares my aunt

made for me. The more dangerous poison is still in the secure section.

Ganipal is in mortal danger. If my aunt has created a potion to poison him, then why and on whose orders? The newspaper article said he was close to death, and if he passes, what will happen to the old factory of nightmares in Ratnagar? Will it be brought back to life?

'I need your help again, Rafi,' I say. 'The nightmares that Aunt Moyna's selling will bring the Citadel down. She has to be stopped. She can't be doing all this alone though, so we will have to be careful who we trust.'

Rafi nods. 'I wonder if your parents knew,' he says. 'What if they found out and wanted to stop her?'

His words make me stop and think. As long as my parents are gone, my aunt is turning my people to darkness, using fear to gain power and wealth. The thought of stepping into the outer world fills me with dread but I am beginning to understand what I have to do.

To stop my aunt from turning our Citadel to darkness, I must go to Ratnagar and save a king I have never met.

CHAPTER TWELVE

The Magic of Dreams

A last-minute trip summons Aunt Moyna away, giving Rafi and me time to put together the next part of our plan. I don't know how far Ratnagar is from the Citadel, but Rafi says there are more ways of getting around than on horseback or foot. He mentions carts and wagons with engines – noisy but speedy. To make it to Ratnagar safely, I may need some of the old dream magic, and, for that, another visit to the library beckons.

It is well past bedtime when we head to the Hall of Mirrors with my father's dream hook in my pocket. As the night teams change shifts, we mingle into the crowd of incoming dream hunters and make our way to the end of the hall. There, we bicker as we look for the mirror connected to Aunt Moyna's office, and I try to convince Rafi he cannot come with me all the way to Ratnagar.

'But we need each other, Mimi. You've never left the Citadel – I can show you how to navigate the outside world and get to the king.'

I shake my head. 'You can't be involved in this. I can claim some kind of kinship with my aunt, but you know what will happen if they catch you.'

But Rafi just laughs. 'Come on, you'll find nothing out by arguing with me all evening.'

'I'm not arguing!'

'Okay, but I'm here now. We can carry on not arguing later. What are we looking for?'

'There is a book of dream magic spells. It might be useful as a way of staying hidden or getting past people when we're no longer in the Citadel.'

With all the other hunters focused on their portals, we step through the liquid glass and into Aunt Moyna's office. My head spins a little as I pass through, and I trip, banging my knee on my aunt's desk.

We open the office door a fraction and listen out. The library is empty, and the corridors are cloaked in darkness. Shards of moonlight slip through the window and cast eerie, multi-coloured glimmers as we pass row after row of bottled dreams.

I spot a light being swept through the windows on the path alongside the library.

'Security rounds,' I whisper to Rafi. The bell tower in the market square tolls ten times. 'Let's keep low.' My ears thrum with the sound of my heartbeat as we crouch down and edge towards the main entrance, where the historical books are stored. I thumb through the catalogue at the end of the aisle and Rafi memorizes the number for the magic textbooks.

There are nightlights along the edges of the room, but these won't help us read the faded titles on the dusty book jackets. Ma once told me the Elders brought only a few books of dream magic with them, as most were destroyed when they were banished from the outer world.

Lalu hops off my shoulder and flitters along the shelves. She must know I need help and she hovers over each book as we follow her path along the row of dusty book jackets. *Architecture, Art, Geography, History* . . . My throat tightens as we search for *Magic*, but we reach *Mathematics* and then *Music*.

Rafi taps my shoulder as Lalu hovers in front of a

gap between two books. Then she flits towards the gap and disappears. Mithi hops off Rafi's shoulder and onto the shelf and, as he pokes his head through the gap, that disappears too then reappears as Mithi pulls it back and gives us a soft tweet. I gasp and put my hand into the space and find myself touching something hard and dusty.

'It's a book, but it has been hidden!' I laugh quietly and grab hold of it, pulling it out gently.

I'm holding a thick, brown-leather book inscribed with gold lettering and alchemy symbols along the spine.

The Magic of Dreams
by Isa Malou

'My great-great-great-great-grandfather,' I whisper, though to me he has always been a faded painting on the library wall, one of the elders who set up our hidden Citadel.

We lay the book on a table and gently leaf through it. The manuscript is written with thick letters and a cursive script which is hard to read, but we marvel at the carefully inked illustrations.

103

'We can use the pictures if we need to,' I say, tucking the book into my school bag.

We hear keys turning in the main door of the library so we half crawl, half run back to my aunt's office, carefully clicking the door closed behind us.

'Let's see if we can find some more clues,' says Rafi. We skirt around the desk and unpick the lock of the drawer. It is filled with files and notebooks.

I dig through the notes on library procedures and ancient statutes.

'Nothing,' I hiss, but as I push the drawer to close it, a flash of pink catches my eye. I dig my hands between the hanging files and pull out an elegant silk-covered scrapbook tucked away at the bottom.

'This looks old,' I whisper, running my hands over the frayed edges of the cover.

There are newspaper cuttings inside and pictures of Aunt Moyna on her travels to faraway lands, places I have never heard of and people I have never seen. On the last page is a yellowed scrap of newspaper, and I recognize the faces, though I have been trying to forget them for the last two years. It's a local rag, *The Daily Citadel*, and it is from two years ago, when my parents were first imprisoned.

A RIGHT ROYAL NIGHTMARE?

Shock as head librarian to be tried for treason

In news that will concern even the most jaded Citadel dweller, the much-respected head of the Library of Forgotten Dreams, Professor Ibrahim Malou, and his wife, Selina, have been charged with orchestrating a treasonous plot to poison the king of Ratnagar, India.

In a case brought by Crown Prince Sakim, it appears that a slowly increasing dose of nightmares has been administered to the prince's father, King Ganipal, over a period of months. Symptoms were first reported on 15 June and culminated in the arrest of Professor and Mrs Malou on their visit to Ratnagar two months later.

Protesting their innocence, Professor Malou said, 'Nightmares have no place in the Citadel. We all know this. My wife and I have never acted in a way that would bring harm to others.'

Yet when interviewed by the Ratnagar investigators, the professor's sister, Moyna Malou, stated that her brother and his wife were in fact collating a collection of nightmares, ostensibly to study the dark side of dreams.

The case against them appears to have been sealed when damning evidence in the form of an empty nightmare-containing bottle, labelled with the king's name, was found in a drawer of Professor Malou's desk. He and his wife have been detained in the palace dungeons at Ratnagar.

If they are convicted, early indications are that a long jail sentence will be imposed to deter others from considering similar crimes in future.

In Professor Malou's absence, the library will be led by Ms Moyna Malou until such time as her niece, Professor Malou's daughter, comes of age.

There are more cuttings from different papers, some old and faded, others newer and more recently filed. I pick up one from the *Ratnagar Express* and start to read but then I stop. My eyes are stinging. Rafi takes it from me gently and carries on.

'"Malou couple arrested for attempted assassination by nightmare. King remains troubled by poor sleep."'

I close my eyes in despair. Why would my parents do something like this? Did they make the bottle we saw in the secure section? Were they just as bad as Aunt Moyna?

'"Couple to be tried for treason and refusal to co-operate . . . *Possible twenty-year sentence in forthcoming historic trial . . .*"'

'I think I have heard enough,' I say.

'Knowledge is power, Mimi. We need to read this,' insists Rafi.

'Okay,' I say, holding my head in my hands as he whispers more headlines.

'"Prince expresses regret at the outrageous behaviour of the Malous" . . . "Malou sister to take over Citadel operations" . . . "Crown Prince Sakim and Moyna Malou announce historic collaboration" . . .'

'Stop, Rafi, I can't bear it—'

And suddenly I realize we have all been fooled. My parents were framed. The act of poisoning for which they were arrested occurred nearly two years ago on the 15 March. My birthday. I was ten that day and my parents took me, as they did every year, into the Forest of Garh to camp under a canopy of trees, dream creatures and stars. They couldn't have been with me in the forest *and* poisoning the king in Ratnagar on the same night. My aunt must have known all this but she has let them rot in a palace dungeon for two years. She has fed me lies, but why? What is she hiding?

Lalu and Mithi whir around the room, as if they sense my anger flaring.

'Let's get out of here.' I stuff some of the newspaper cuttings into my bag and some envelopes filled with letters. I'll read them later. Right now, my mind is on fire because everything I have held to be true these last two years was a lie.

CHAPTER THIRTEEN

Calm Among the Chaos

When I am safely back home, I open my bag. In a thin, worn, brown envelope are a pile of yellowed papers. They are all handwritten letters, and my mouth falls open when I see they are addressed to me. Written to me, but hidden from me. I carefully lay one of them out on my bed and spread it flat, hands shaking with furious disbelief.

Our dearest Mimi,

We have been delayed in Ratnagar on what appears to be a misunderstanding. The king and his son seem to think we wish them ill, though nothing could be further from the truth. We have been appointed a legal advisor who seems at best uninterested, at worst conspiring against us.

Whatever anyone says, know that we love you and have not abandoned you.

Your loving

Ma and Papa x

PS Please take care of Jala.

PPS Do not forget your studies. Hard work and dedication are the sure way to lift yourself out of the troubles that life can sometimes bring.

My emotions fight for my attention. Confusion gallops in first. My parents knew there was a plot and tried to warn me, but I was told lies which turned me against them. The feeling of guilt I've carried around with me now turns to pride in my parents. Even in their troubles they were worried for me. As I read on, the letters become more desperate, more angry and finally bitter.

I stroke the outline of their words, wondering how they kept their spirits up enough to reassure me that they would return home, but the final letter sends a chill down my spine. It is from only last week, dated the day Jamal came to the Citadel.

Dearest Mimi,

It is likely our letters are not reaching you, but it feels vital we continue to write and explain. We are pleased to hear from our guards in Ratnagar that you are safe and well. This is the only glimmer of light in our very dark world.

We have been forsaken and forgotten, tricked into coming here and wrongly accused of heinous acts. Things are not going well, and we have lost a legal battle to clear our names and return home. We will be sentenced at next month's meeting of the Council of Elders, and we fear the worst.

We have no faith in your aunt, who has conspired against us and is intent on weaponizing dreams. It saddens us beyond measure that we might not see you grow into a young woman and cannot explain to you what has happened. We will never give up trying to get back to you, but, should we fail, we hope you will one day understand and forgive us for our absence.

With love always,
    Ma and Papa x

They never stopped trying to reach me. They never gave up on me. They are innocent.

I grip the paper tightly and finally let the ball of sadness rise up and the tears I have held down for the last two years spill out. Everything I have been led to believe about my parents is a lie, and I am angry at myself for letting my aunt turn me against them.

Having removed my parents, Aunt Moyna is creating nightmares to get rid of the king of Ratnagar. The thought fills me with bitter disgust. But why is she doing this? Does she want to establish the nightmare trade again? Why sell terror and hatred when dreams can offer so much benefit?

I pull back the rug at the end of my bed and lift the loose floorboard.

The gold coin from the bag of money Jamal bought glimmers in the dappled light of morning. I trace my finger across the writing on it . . . *Ratnagar*, where a much-loved old king will give way to a nightmare-loving prince. *Ratnagar*, the place where my parents are. The place where they were framed, jailed, trapped.

I must follow their path, and to do that will take more courage than I think I have.

I must persuade a king of the danger he is in. *He* is

the key to stopping all of this.

I pack some spare clothes and some loose change. Finally, I return to the hiding place under the floorboard. Raging and twisting inside a dirty green bottle are the nightmare threads my aunt created to haunt my dreams. They hurl themselves at the stopper, itching to get out.

A chill seizes me as I wrap the bottle in a scarf and push it to the bottom of my bag, ignoring the furious dark curses and protestations which are fighting to poison me. *I will leave the Citadel*, I tell myself – but how and when will be the first of many trials ahead of me.

The next morning, instead of class, we are attending a dream creature ceremony for one of the younger students, Simya Sooli, in the dream creature sanctuary. Rafi and I are among the first to arrive.

Glittering birds of all colours and sizes flit through the branches above us, scattering cherry blossom onto our shoulders like pink and white confetti. The grass beneath our feet is a rich, verdant carpet, fed by spring water from the plateau which rolls across the spine of India.

'I read the letters from my parents, Rafi.' My eyes still sting at the thought of them stuck in a dungeon, losing their hope and their courage. 'We have to leave tonight.'

We fall quiet as Madame Noori, guardian of the dream creatures, takes her place at the front. Madame Noori's eyes are deep like the ocean. Grey and blue with flecks of green, they change with her mood and this morning they are dark as thunderclouds. Perhaps she senses the changes afoot, but as Simya appears the guardian's expression softens and she calls the young girl to join her at the front. Simya is the grand-daughter of the chief justice of the Citadel. Having completed the primary dream-catching programme, she will receive her dream creature today.

'Bring your bag and meet me after school at the bread stall we stopped at yesterday,' I whisper.

Rafi gives a slight nod.

Madame Noori flicks back her soft curls of hair revealing a golden sparrow on her left shoulder. It hops to her wrist and then flutters down to the stone table and looks up at Simya, who gasps with delight. The bird has a soft golden glow, with feathers that are almost transparent. Madame Noori touches the sparrow's breast with her dream hook, and a throbbing gentle glow radiates out from the bird's body. 'This is Chirya,' she says, 'a catcher of gentle thoughts and the finest of dreams. May your companion bring you happiness, and may you comfort and nourish her in return.'

Simya holds out her finger and the bird flitters up to land on it. She gently strokes the creature's head. 'I can barely feel its weight,' she whispers.

Madame Noori encourages Simya to release the bird for her first hunt. Slowly, the young girl holds out her arm, and Chirya flutters up, circling above her head a few times then zipping higher over the treeline, over the wall of the Citadel and away, to catch the forgotten dreams of the people in the outer world.

'She will return by nightfall,' says Madame Noori. 'Keep your window open and a soft nest of leaves and feathers ready.' Simya nods and skitters back to her friends.

I give Rafi a grim smile.

If all goes to plan, by nightfall we will be gone.

CHAPTER FOURTEEN

A Change of Guard

Tension crackles through the Citadel at the end of the school day, leaving an eerie silence in its trail, as if the world has ground to a halt. Then, at first from afar, we hear a distant rumble from the forest outside the Citadel walls. It grows and grows, closer and closer, into the thunderous arrival of soldiers from Ratnagar who fill the market square with the clatter and clang of horse hooves and shields.

I see Madame Noori at the school gates. Her face unusually red and flustered, she sends the younger children back into the classroom. Now Monsieur Julin has joined her and they huddle and whisper. Looking across the square to the vast windows along the length

115

of the library, I see Aunt Moyna inside, returned from her trip. A red-cloaked man is standing next to her. It is Jamal, the envoy from Ratnagar.

I dodge my way between the crowds and arrive, breathless, at the entrance of the library, which suddenly seems full of soldiers. A moment later Madame Noori is at my side and together we edge our way forward. Madame Noori pats my shoulder and hushes me softly as we watch Aunt Moyna come striding along the length of the library towards us, directing the soldiers. Her voice ricochets off the shelves.

'Be careful! These are very valuable,' says my aunt as the soldiers bring out nightmares from the secure section. They work fast, pulling bottles roughly off the shelves and placing them into wooden boxes.

Suddenly there is a crash. One of the bottles has fallen to the floor. It's all too fast to stop what happens next: the stopper pops off, the nightmare leaks out with a hiss at first, then starts to come together into the monstrous and horrifying form of a gigantic green lion, its yellow eyes as large as dinner plates and teeth dripping with blood. It roars and races through the library sending the soldiers scattering. One of them is too slow and screams as the nightmare passes through him. His face drains of colour as the vision rushes on, towards the doorway, where it finally fizzles away in the sunlight.

'Moyna, why are you removing the secure items?' asks Madame Noori. 'You know the protocol. Two senior dream threaders should be present for a procedure such as this. Not these . . . outsiders.'

Aunt Moyna makes her way to the entrance. She is carrying one of the boxes. The bottles in it are old and dusty. Their shapes are intricately carved with terrifying creatures and the caps are made of pure gold.

'Times have changed, Hira. We need to rotate our stock, keep up with demand.'

Madame Noori snorts. 'You think the outer world will want us to return to the dark arts? The kings of Ratnagar have protected our trade for generations, but only while we traded in *dreams*. What will King Ganipal say about this?'

'Ganipal is dying, and though his heir recognizes the danger in nightmares, he also sees their power and potential.'

Madame Noori gives her a look of disdain, but it is lost on my aunt, who strides onwards, stacking the box on the pile that will be transported to Ratnagar.

117

'You can't do this!' I shout in vain at the heavy-footed strangers hauling boxes filled to the brim with glass bottles. Their carelessness sends scores of dreams crashing to the ground as they pass through the library. As the glass splinters, the dream threads emerge, soft at first then fizzing as they sense freedom, but they are soon torched by beams of sunlight and fade away. My heart rages. The heritage of what is being lost, its value, cannot be counted.

'Please, Aunt Moyna, tell them to be more careful,' I say.

Aunt Moyna lowers her voice when she sees me, but her eyes are cold and focused. 'There are simply too many, my petal, and I no longer have any need of them. We will focus on more powerful, more potent dreams instead.'

'To be clear, Moyna, you mean nightmares,' says Madame Noori with fresh contempt.

'We will start afresh, Hira. The Citadel needs fresh trade. Look around you: our home is falling into decay.'

'Yes, but this goes against all our ideals and traditions. It is madness,' counters Madame Noori. She turns to face the crowd of onlookers that has gathered at the library entrance. 'Citizens of the Citadel! Children!

118

Today is not a good day. These heathens are destroying our sacred space.'

'Watch your mouth, woman,' shouts one of the soldiers.

Kala lifts off and circles the delicately painted dome of the library, cawing and screeching with relish.

Madame Noori stands in the entrance, her hands on her hips, blocking the passage of soldiers and nightmares. 'You have no right, Moyna,' she says. 'Only the guardian of the phoenix can direct the contents of the library, and since the pheonix Tala does not recognize you as his guardian but remains in the mountains, it would seem you are but a temporary custodian of what is stored in this building.'

'You should leave before I run out of patience and have you all removed by force. Permanently,' growls my aunt, and she starts shooing us away.

Seizing my chance in the confusion, I slide unnoticed into a gap behind the nearest shelf. The library houses dreams that could help so many people. They don't belong to Aunt Moyna. They don't belong to anyone. I can't let my aunt take them.

A librarian's jacket is draped over the back of a chair. I pull it on and in among the hullabaloo of soldiers I

119

now look like another minion working to sort the dreams into 'keep' and 'toss' piles. I work my way to the special shelf where historical and particularly valuable dreams are kept. I skirt past two soldiers and locate a group of the most precious dream threads in the collection: I reach for a bottle of grade two, with long-lasting threads of joy which we sometimes add to potions for those suffering from longstanding anxiety or sadness. I reach for a bottle. Its threads glitter blue and shimmer with promise, and I feel hope surge just from touching the glass but as I lift it off the shelf, my bag swings and knocks another bottle to the floor. It sends a hollow ring skittering along the cavernous library walls and, for a moment, time seems to stand still and my heartbeat thunders.

Then a shout from my aunt. 'Someone's in the aisles at the back. Go check!'

I hear the stomp of soldiers' boots. 'It came from the side overlooking the square,' one of them shouts.

In desperation, I pull off the cap to the bottle I picked up and a couple of threads inch out. I blow on them gently and they transform into dozens of blue-winged butterflies which flutter into the library, distracting the soldiers, who stop and fall silent in wonder at the floating dreams which settle on their foreheads and paint stories in their minds. But it's only a matter of time before the dreams are over . . . I can't stay here.

I climb to a windowsill and ease myself through onto the outer ledge. My head spins as I look down at the fall below me.

An edge of scarlet cloak flashes behind me, and a young red-faced soldier puffs his face as he spots me.

'It's a girl!' he shouts. 'She's trying to get away!'

Lalu flitters around my hair, nervous and excitable.

'I know, little one,' I say.

The soldier is already at the window; he reaches out to me – his hand grasps my arm – but I shake him off and, with my bag held close to my chest, I shut my eyes and jump.

CHAPTER FIFTEEN

When All Is Dark Around You

I land on the cloth roof of a market stall. It sags and groans as I fall off onto a mass of pots and pans below. A trickle of blood runs down my leg from a graze on my knee, but I can stand. Nothing broken. The stallholder curses as hc pulls himself out from under the crumpled awning of his stall.

A couple of soldiers run out of the main door of the library.

'Find the girl!'

I toss away the librarian's jacket and pull my scarf around my face. The man whose stall I fell on looms tall and large over me. He is a wall of a man, and his brow is furrowed. My cheeks flush pink in embarrassment and fear, but his face softens as he crouches down.

'Go. Get away from her. Somewhere she can never reach you,' he whispers.

As I stand up, I hear a shout. I've been spotted by one of the soldiers looking out from the library window. He shouts again and points in my direction.

'Seize her!'

I start to run towards the middle of the square, but as I pass the bread stall a hand reaches out, grabs my elbow and pulls me back into a corner.

'Ouch!' I say, trying to pull free, but the grip tightens, fingers digging tightly into my arm.

'You must have done something really bad this time, Mimi.'

I look round and see it's Rafi, and almost hug him with relief.

'Quick! We've got to get out of the Citadel. Now!'

He nods. 'I brought my bag and I have Mithi.'

The shoppers and market traders cluster together in groups, leaving a way through the throng for the prince's emissary as he marches across the square. They look down, not wanting to stand out or be questioned. How did these once proud citizens become so meek?

Rafi and I cloak ourselves in the shadow of an alleyway and wait. A drip of water from a drainpipe falls on my shoulder and I shudder.

'What's the plan?' asks Rafi.

I bite my lip. 'Well, um, get to Mumbai, and from there to Ratnagar and save the king from poisoning. If he dies, my parents are doomed. How we get to Mumbai . . . well, I'm still not sure about the details. But you can leave me when we get to Mumbai. Your friends will be happy to see you.'

'None of this leaving me behind,' he says.

'You've been through enough. This is something *I* must do.'

'Do you think that will be easy? You've never even left the Citadel.'

'I know, but I can't let Aunt Moyna destroy everything I love. My home and my family.'

He puts his hands together and pleads. 'Let me help you. I know the outside world.'

A loud trumpeting sound interrupts our fizzing argument. It reverberates around the market square causing everyone to fall silent. All eyes turn towards the steps of the council building, where my aunt is standing next to a man in a black cloak and white wig.

It is Saqib Sooli, the chief justice of the Citadel, Simya's grandfather. He seems to be arguing with my aunt, but shrugs as he realizes we are overpowered, allowing himself to be ushered away by Suri and other dream technicians.

A richly dressed soldier comes forward and stands where the chief justice had stood. He looks out into the square and begins to speak in a voice that is harsh and angry.

'I speak on behalf of Crown Prince Sakim of Ratnagar.' It is Jamal and he directs his soldiers to mill through the crowd. 'The kingdom of Ratnagar offers to reopen trade with the Citadel, to bring wealth and security to your people once again.'

A low murmur starts swimming through the market square mixed in with an occasional louder voice of protest, but opposition is soon quelled as soldiers take out truncheons and disperse people into smaller groups.

'For too long,' continues Jamal, 'the Library of Forgotten Dreams has become a myth, a stale story with no relevance or significance in the world at large.'

My heart races as I look around. Soldiers scatter through the crowd, on the lookout. I pull my hood over my head and look down.

My aunt takes over from Jamal.

'Today is a great day,' she says. 'The kingdom of Ratnagar has asked us to broaden our trade in dream craft. There are many who would pay good money for our fast and efficient nightmare potions to settle wars or overcome traitors – traitors like my brother and sister-in-law.'

Just then Suri returns and whispers in Aunt Moyna's ear. I feel a chill run through my heart as my aunt casts her gaze across the square, and for a moment she catches my eye.

The soldiers from Ratnagar are on the hunt and I am their prey.

Rafi tugs at my sleeve. 'Come on, before they find us.'

I follow him through the backstreets, keeping our heads down and our eyes alert. In a small side street we pass a metal gate to a garden and spy a washing line. I point to the clothes pegged out to dry.

'Okay, I'll keep a lookout, in case—' begins Rafi, catching onto my plan, but before he can even finish his sentence I've leaped over the gate and am pulling a linen dress and man's tunic off the line, throwing them over my shoulder. As we turn to run away, we hear the back door opening and a woman shrieking to someone inside the house.

'Thieves!' she shouts, but her voice is lost to the wind as Rafi and I run through hidden passages that only we know, until we are near the edge of the Citadel, where we cram into one of the lookout posts close to the outer wall. In another minute we have assumed our disguises. If the soldiers are looking for a pair of children wearing the cobalt-blue uniform of the Citadel school, they won't give a second glance to someone garbed in a sack of a dress and her companion wearing a black tunic about two sizes too big.

We emerge from the lookout post and keeping to the shadows and alleyways of the Citadel we make our way towards the main entrance.

As we near the carts and horses stationed near the main gate, a hushed voice makes me stop in my tracks.

'Mimi, is that you?'

Normally, the harsh stare that Madame Griffin doles out to unsuspecting children is enough to freeze anyone to the spot, but right now her face is grey with worry.

'Madame Griffin,' I stammer, 'we need to get to Ratnagar . . . we don't have time to . . .'

'I know, I understand.' She nods and we look at each other wide-eyed.

'You won't stop us?' I say, wondering if we can trust her.

'I should be coming with you, but I must stay and find a way to protect the library. There are spies in our ranks and I do not know who to trust. You must help King Ganipal before it is too late for him – and for your parents.'

'Did you know they were innocent?'

She puts her arm around me awkwardly, and I see her eyes mist a little. 'I didn't want to believe the rumours, but the evidence was strong. Whatever the outcome, I know they are good people.'

'I am going to clear my parents' name,' I tell her.

'To do that, we need the king, and Ratnagar is far away,' says Rafi.

'Yes, indeed. It's many, many miles to the north,' says Madame Griffin. 'The journey ahead of you is long.'

'We'll find a way,' I say. 'I don't know how, but we will.' My brain whirs at the thought of the journey we are about to undertake.

'I have sent word to my brother, Amir—' She pauses as Rafi sniggers, and purses her lips. 'Yes, Rafi, I have a sibling, and he is perfectly amiable.' I push down my own smile as Madame Griffin continues: 'Make your way south, down into the valley. My brother runs a guest house for travellers on the outskirts of Songra, a small village at the base of the plateau. Traders often stop off there on their way in and out of the Citadel, and Amir has his ear to the ground. Ever since your parents . . .' Madame Griffin looks at me a moment. 'Well, the locals have become less trusting and some may be in league with your aunt. Amir will help you get to Mumbai, and from there you can board a train north. That route will be faster than going directly by road.'

The colour drains from my face at the thought of the outside world.

'It's okay, Mimi,' says Rafi. 'I have friends in Mumbai who will help us.'

A burst of *clinks* and *clanks* from metal boots and horses' hooves shatters the calm in the streets outside and we fall silent.

'We should leave, Madame Griffin. I don't want you to get into trouble for helping us.'

'Have no fear of that,' she says with a grim smile.

'To luminous thoughts, Madame, and may we see each other soon.'

'May your dreams shine ever brightly, Mimi Malou, and yours too, Rafi. I know you will be a great help.'

As we make to leave, Madame Griffin places a hand on my shoulder.

'Wait,' she says, removing a golden necklace from around her neck and fastening it around mine. The chain is finely twisted and glimmers in the sunlight. Hanging from it is a small egg-shaped pendant with a line across the middle. I feel uncomfortable about accepting such a generous gift and start to pull at the ends of it, but she stops me. 'No. This pendant belonged to my mother. She told me it should be used only in a situation of extreme peril. You may have need of it.'

I shake my head and lift the chain away from my neck. 'This is your family's treasure, Madame. I can't take it.'

She wraps her hands around mine. 'Yes, you can and you must. You may need it.'

'Is it magic?' I ask her.

Madame Griffin smiles and gently lifts the golden pendant. 'Inside this capsule is a powerful dream. It will bring you hope and light when none is left. It will bring you happiness again when all is dark around you. Twist and separate the halves.' She brings her face close. 'Use it wisely. It will only work once.'

CHAPTER SIXTEEN

Hunted

A raven swoops low above us, so close I see its head turn. My face flashes red as I recognize the black, beady eyes.

'Watch out for the spies above,' I say, turning my face away. It is Carab, Suri's dream creature. Today he is filled with bitter, harsh green and silver dreams. He must feed on the same anger and darkness that has consumed the soul of his human.

'We'll never make it out of the Citadel with their dream creatures on the lookout,' says Rafi.

Our own dream creatures cower, sensing our fear, hiding in our coats lest they give us away. I feel a tightness in my throat as we approach the gates of the

Citadel, filled with citadel guards checking papers and ticking names off a list.

A group of soldiers passes close by to us. 'Move, peasants, don't you know who I am?'

I look up and stare into the stone-cold face of Jamal. He doesn't recognize me.

'Why are you here?' he asks. 'Where are your exit passes?'

Rafi shuffles his feet and coughs. 'We are helping move the bottles from the library, ready for transportation.'

I reach inside my pocket and put my hand around my dream hook, ready to poke the sharp end of it into Jamal's arm if I need to, but he nods and walks off, followed by a trail of soldiers of a lower rank. Unlike Jamal's, their red cloaks are faded and worn, their boots scuffed, and their faces marked by scars and bruises, signs of previous combat.

We crouch behind teetering stacks of crates waiting to be loaded onto carts. The sky turns from blue to crimson-orange as the sun sinks below the Citadel wall. Behind us, in the square, the vast windows of the library still glint in the late-afternoon light, but the coloured bottles of dreams are scattered and the rainbow has faded.

132

'Ready?' I whisper to Rafi, but as I start to move, the hairs on my neck stand on end. Someone is right behind us. Slowly we turn and look up into the face of a guard looking down at us. She can't be much older than me, but her face is thin, no doubt from the meagre rations they are given, and her eyes lined by fatigue.

'Hm, you look familiar,' she says, and her face turns from me to Rafi as she tries to place us. My heart is beating so loudly I fear it may give us away. After a tense moment, she decides to let us through and waves her hand for us to pass, but just as we are stepping away from her, Lalu peeks her head out of my pocket. A crooked smile spreads across the guard's face and she grabs my arm.

'Ha, I do know you – you're Mimi Malou! Your aunt is looking for you.'

With all the force he can muster, Rafi stamps hard on her foot and Mithi shoots towards her head and pecks at her ear. She screams in pain, pulling away her hand and freeing me from her clutches.

'You must have really come down hard on that foot!' I whisper.

Rafi smiles. 'I can take care of myself,' he says, 'and my friends.'

133

'Stop them!' the woman shouts, raising the alarm and hobbling towards us. Her voice nearly swallowed by the trundling of cartwheels, but a Ratnagar soldier turns his head and sees us and joins in the chase, pulling out his sword. We are just seconds from passing through the Citadel gate; its archway looms majestically over us, but gatekeepers are preparing to close it and, once they do, we won't be able to escape. There is only one thing left we can do and my skin crawls at the thought of it.

I pull the bottle of nightmares from my bag.

'You create a distraction then run ahead,' I tell Rafi. I show him the bottle.

Rafi stares at me a moment. 'Be careful. Those threads were made for you, so they might be keener on your mind than theirs.'

'I know, but they won't be expecting it and I'll move away fast.'

Rafi steps into the light and faces the soldier and the guard pursuing us. 'Hey, you with the red cloak, you're not wanted here!' he shouts, ducking into the maze of crates.

The soldier grunts and I coil into the shadows, untwisting the bottle stopper.

'We're not afraid of you!' Rafi's words thread themselves over the boxes, taunting the soldier, and I

134

can tell he's trying to sound brave, but his voice has a higher pitch than normal.

'I'll skewer you with my sword when I catch you, toe rag!' shouts the man, who thunders towards the sound of Rafi's voice.

But the guard glances my way and spots me lurking – 'Over here!' – but the leer on her face creases in confusion when she catches sight of the bottle of ghostly green threads. I pull away the stopper and the nightmares hiss and bubble as they race out, screaming wild curses and odious threats as they fly towards the soldier and the guard.

'What is this?' Their eyes bulge as they try to flick the nightmares away, but the threads are hungry and unrelenting, burrowing into their skin.

'Make it stop!' says the woman, and my stomach twists with guilt.

Rafi pulls my arm. 'Quick! Leave them. We need to get out before their minds clear.'

Holding our bags under our cloaks and looking down we pull ourselves up and away.

A local trader is unloading a delivery of herbs and spices to the Citadel. The scents wafting out of the wooden casks spark thoughts of my mother's food, the warmth and comfort so far away now. It reminds me of the mountain ahead of us, and the time we don't have.

'You're sure about this?' asks Rafi.

'Never surer,' I say as we creep behind the cart and horse and cross the Citadel gateway.

We are out.

We are free.

As we tread the path that leads into the trees, the snap of a twig under my feet fills a void and I realize we have been surrounded by silence. I gaze back along the path. Behind us, where there should be walls and crowds, there are ghost trees stretching into the darkness. Here, the only signs of dream magic are the flickers of light that dart through the trees above. Woodpeckers and pigeons, magpies and sparrows – dream creatures are watching us, and I hope they will light our way.

CHAPTER SEVENTEEN

Strangers in a Strange Land

Our path from the Citadel to Songra leads us south, through a web of trees and the dream creatures who hide within it, descending into a valley where the roads and rivers lead to the ocean. We walk in single file, catching glimpses of the villages and hamlets down below as we watch our step through the forest. At times the path splits, but we stick to the larger branch each time, the one the traders must use to move goods to and from the Citadel. Soon my ears prickle to the sound of horses' hooves closing in from behind us.

'Could be a trader,' whispers Rafi.

'Or soldiers,' I say. 'Whoever it is, we can't outrun them.'

We find a fallen branch. It is large enough to cause

a cart to tip, and my hands slip and slide with sweat as we haul it across the path to block the way out of the forest. Then we hide behind the trunk of a large acacia tree as we catch our breath and wait. I clutch the bark and scratch the rough peel to calm the whirlwind of fear inside my mind.

'If it's a trader we could hop in their cart,' says Rafi.

'If it's not, we have to hope they don't bring their ravens.'

Lalu and Mithi hide in our arms as we peer through the swishing leaves onto the path in front of us.

The sound of a horse-drawn cart comes closer, the wheels clattering and complaining over the rocky ground. It comes into view, an old man driving it, the trader who was unloading his wares at the gate. He's too busy swatting the flies that buzz around his turban to notice us, as his horse, a tired-looking dark bay, trots along at a leisurely pace.

'Whoa there, Nargis,' says the trader as he pulls the horse to a stop. 'What have we got here, girl?'

He's so close now I can smell him, a mix of sweat and spice, with eyes that are quick and suspicious, darting around for signs of trouble. My feet itch to run away, but my mind forces me into a tight crouch. Soon the old man realizes he must move the branch to move along the path, so with grumblings and mumblings, words my parents would never even let me hear, the trader dismounts. I feel a knot of guilt as he walks around his cart with a bit of a hobble in his left knee and stops, hands on his hips, by the branch lying across the path.

'Funny how that got here,' he says, 'but no matter. If old Del Aziz wants to get home to his wife, he'd better get moving, eh, Nargis?'

While he is distracted, we move behind the trees until we are lined up with the back of the cart. The chance of a lift down to the valley would be a welcome respite from being alone on the open road. But as we prepare to move, our ears catch a more alarming signal.

The angry gallop of Ratnagar's finest horses approaches, bringing the worst possible combination of people. Suri and the soldier we threw nightmare threads over canter towards Del Aziz, coming to a halt beside the fallen log, with Carab, Suri's raven, following behind them like a malicious black kite. The soldier glides off his horse with well-practised grace. Suri, less accustomed to riding, catches her foot and trips, falling flat on her backside.

Del Aziz covers an amused smile with his hand as the soldier helps Suri up.

'Evening,' he says. 'Trouble in the Citadel, is there?'

'Escaped convicts. Have you seen them?'

Rafi and I mouth our disbelief. *Convicts?*

'Haven't seen anyone,' says Del Aziz. 'What do they look like, these convicts, in case I come across them – the apprehension of whom I presume leads to some kind of reward?' The three of them proceed to talk in a quiet huddle and, though I struggle to hear what they say, a smattering of alarming words drifts over to us: 'dangerous' . . . 'thieves' . . . 'treason'.

Suddenly Del Aziz lets out a deep guffaw, throwing his head back and holding his belly. 'What, you're looking for a couple of *kids?* Moyna Malou sends her chief technician and a Ratnagar soldier because she wants to find a pair of young dream hunters?'

'Careful, Del Aziz,' warns Suri. 'You will find yourself without a trading licence with such insolence.'

'Okay, okay, I'll keep my eye out for them. Now, help me get this blasted log off the path, will you?'

As they pass to the front of the cart, Rafi and I take our chance. Soft as butterflies, we lift ourselves into the back of the cart and dive under the tarpaulin. Luckily Carab is flittering over Del Aziz, cawing angrily at him, but Nargis notices us. She gives a whinny, but with Del Aziz hauling one end of the log, the soldier the other and Suri bossing them both around, the horse's warning goes unheeded, and before any of them looks back our way, we have curled ourselves tight as fists into the gaps between the casks.

'If you spot them, send word to the Citadel. My raven will follow you,' says Suri.

I slap my hand over my mouth to cloak a moan of despair, but Del Aziz is having none of it.

'Pish and nonsense! If I see them, I'll send a message the usual way. And don't forget my reward!' he calls as Suri and the guard ride off.

'What's the "usual way"?' whispers Rafi.

I shrug. 'Carrier pigeon? Who knows.'

The cart judders as Del Aziz hauls himself back into his seat and, soon enough, we are on our way. The path seems to twist and turn as the cart turns this way and that over a thousand sharp stones as it rumbles down into the valley.

'Do you think Songra is much further?' I say.

'Probably not. You do look a bit green though,' whispers Rafi.

I feel my stomach crunching and hold down a retch. 'I need air. Do you think we can get out?'

Rafi carefully lifts up the edge of the tarpaulin and

I stick my nose over the edge of the cart and breathe in lungfuls of cool air. As soon as I can, I pull the tarpaulin back into place, hoping my insides will keep themselves under control.

After a while longer Del Aziz's mood seems to lift and he starts to sing a ditty about a girl who lived in the city of stars. The ground is more level now, marking the bottom of the valley.

Sliding between the cargo, Rafi and I move towards the back of the cart. Nargis must sense the shifting around and whinnies in protest, but Del Aziz carries on singing, after giving the horse a few choice words.

We inch ourselves over the back of the cart, clutching onto a metal bar running along the panel, but keeping ourselves low so Del Aziz can't see us from the front. As I look to the side, I can see the plateau rising high above us, and a lush, green meadow below. The path is broader now and winds towards a babbling river.

'We'll jump off as he takes the corner,' I say, pointing to an approaching sharp bend in the path.

Rafi nods. 'Good idea. There are some tall shrubs there for us to blend into.'

As the cart begins to turn, I use my bag to cushion the fall and roll off the path into the shrubbery. Rafi lands awkwardly and seems to be in pain as he tumbles into the grass on the other side of the path, Mithi fluttering along behind him. I want to rush over but Del Aziz pulls up his horse and comes to a stop.

My heart is thundering as the trader walks around to the back of the cart and lifts the loose tarpaulin. He looks around, then tightens it back up.

'Strange day today, girl. I wish I'd never set eyes on the Citadel,' says Del Aziz. 'They're more trouble than they're worth up there. All high and mighty with their dream magic.'

Nargis snorts and shakes her head as the old man suddenly looks in the direction Rafi fell and rolled away.

Lalu flits out of my pocket and, as she hovers in front of me, her dream-filled belly gives me an idea.

'Quick, Lalu, create a distraction,' I say.

My dream creature gives me a tiny nod and zips over to land on Nargis's head.

I used to wonder about animals and if they have dreams, but having watched my aunt's cat Frou-Frou flicking her tail and meowing in her sleep I can only assume they must do. Lalu opens her slender beak and drops all the threads she holds over Nargis. The horse neighs then starts to canter along the path as if sleepwalking.

Del Aziz's attention is pulled back to his cart, and he hobbles after his horse. He doesn't spot Lalu as she flies along the treeline making her way back to me. As soon as he is back behind his horse and heading down to the bridge, Rafi lifts his head above the long grass.

'Is it sore?' I ask, nodding towards his right arm, which looks stiff and bruised. Mithi sits on Rafi's shoulder, looking a little forlorn.

'Didn't do myself justice with that jump, but I didn't want you to be the only one with war wounds,' he says, pointing to my knee with a grin. 'I'm usually pretty nifty.'

We start walking towards Songra. It is early evening by the time we reach the edge of the village in the valley beneath the Citadel.

'Let's get our story straight first,' I say, pausing near the entrance

'We are failed dream hunters, thrown out of the Citadel and making our way back to Mumbai. Almost true,' says Rafi.

I am about to nod in agreement when a hand grabs my shoulder. I freeze. 'You're a hard one to catch, Mimi Malou.'

CHAPTER EIGHTEEN

A Familiar Pair of Eyes

I turn my head towards the hand, and find myself looking up at a tall, wiry man with a greying beard and a strangely familiar pair of eyes. I am ready to make my excuses and deny everything, when he smiles and grabs our hands, shaking them warmly.

'Who are you?' I scratch my head and smile at him awkwardly.

The man bows his head. 'I am Amir. An innkeeper to some, but a dream threader until five years ago, when I met my wife and left the Citadel.' Amir gives us a conspiratorial wink. 'Leena Griffin is my older sister.'

We look at each other and smile.

'So, can you also wither a child's resolve in two minutes flat?' I ask.

'Ha! Sadly, no. That is a skill I never acquired.' Amir chuckles. 'Though I too have been on the receiving end of her stare, on more than one occasion.'

I stiffen as a woman walks past. She looks at us with interest then continues on her way, but not before giving Amir a curt nod.

Amir lowers his voice. 'These are odd times. Your parents came and went – of course, you know that. Then it was quiet until your aunt started letting in all kinds of folk from Ratnagar.'

My throat goes tight. 'Do you know what happened to my parents?'

'They said your father wanted to turn the Citadel to the dark side, to take the power of nightmares back into Ratnagar. Your mother seems to have been a willing accomplice in it all, but . . .' Amir purses his lips.

I clench my fists. 'Those stories are wrong. I know it, but I need to prove it to King Ganipal.'

He pats my shoulder. 'I hope you are right. From the messages my sister has sent, we must get you to Ratnagar double-quick!'

Following Amir, we keep our steps swift and our ears

alert to the conversations and questions around us. There is a lot of talk of Ratnagar, how soldiers have been coming through the village for weeks. Ratnagar is hundreds of miles away, the journey is long, so people realize there is something afoot.

Amir takes us to the Cozee Inn, an old, whitewashed building with a verandah running across the front and large wooden doors that lead onto an inner courtyard where a fountain softly trickles. A few guests are making their way to their rooms. There are no red-robed soldiers of Ratnagar, or white-coated library technicians, but Rafi and I tread as softly as we can, following Amir past the guest house lobby and into the staff quarters.

His wife, Alia, a soft woman with beautiful cat-like eyes, welcomes us with a hug. Her gesture makes me realize how much I have missed the warmth of trusted grown-ups.

'Have some food, and perhaps you might like to freshen up,' she says, bringing food and drink to the table. 'And we'll get you some clothes that fit.'

Our bellies are grateful for the hot, spiced potatoes and some crispy flatbread washed down with ice-cold soda. We scoff it down in big, hungry mouthfuls, while Lalu and Mithi set off to hunt dreams in this strange, new world. After we have eaten and changed into the clean clothes Alia brought for us, we explain our plan.

'Mumbai is a few hours' ride from here. There are no trains, and the road is rocky and dangerous,' says Amir.

My tummy twists a little as it remembers the journey from the Citadel in the back of the cart, but I have to ignore it.

'We have no choice. Time is running out for the king of Ratnagar,' I say.

'I have heard he is gravely unwell,' says Amir. 'He is a good man by all accounts, much loved by his people, and an important factor in the balance of power in the Northern Kingdoms.'

'From what we know, his son wants to restart the nightmare trade in Ratnagar,' says Rafi.

Amir shakes his head. 'History repeating itself. And if the king dies, a dangerous man will step into powerful shoes.'

'The prince is acting like he is already in charge, by the sound of it,' I say. 'He sent his emissary and a whole lot of soldiers to start taking bottled nightmares back to Ratnagar.'

'I have seen them – some stayed here only last night.'

Amir pulls out a map from his desk and points to a dot in the middle of the upside-down triangle that is India. Songra is so small, its name is barely readable. He moves his finger westwards towards the large metropolis of Mumbai. 'The fastest way to Ratnagar is the overnight train from Mumbai. I can drop you on the outskirts of the city.'

After we have thanked Alia again and said our goodbyes, Amir leads us around the back of the guest house to a yard where his horse and cart are already loaded up. There is a bench fitted at the front, long enough for Rafi and me to squeeze on alongside him, and before we know it we have climbed up and set off with our few belongings and a tiffin each of food for the journey.

As we trundle out of the village, the night drapes itself around us as cool air sinks down from the plateau above. My heart feels stretched, as if an elastic band is pulling me back to the Citadel when I know my path must go in the opposite direction. I feel a sting of tears but wipe my face as we catch up with another cart that's travelling slowly.

It's Del Aziz and his wife. They slow down and gesture to Amir as we pass by.

'What a fine evening,' says Del Aziz as he scans our

cart. 'So, you are driving your visitors around now, are you, Amir?'

'These are my niece and nephew, visiting from Barodra,' says Amir. Rafi and I keep our faces still as water, snuggling Lalu and Mithi safely in our coat pockets, but Del Aziz is not content with the lie.

'Oh? They're not from the Citadel, then?' He pauses and gives me a long stare. 'I heard Moyna Malou has a reward out for some thieving kids who escaped the Citadel, one of them quite special,' he says. 'You wouldn't know anything about that, would you, children?' He looks at his wife and raises an eyebrow.

A bead of sweat breaks out on my forehead, and it takes all my resolve not to wipe it.

Mrs Del Aziz rolls her eyes. 'Such nonsense,' she says. 'I never much liked Moyna, truth be told. Let's not get caught up in whatever nonsense the Citadel is cooking up.'

Rafi and I give each other a furtive side-eye glance as Del Aziz and his wife continue on their way.

'Good evening to you, both, may tomorrow bring you good fortune,' says Amir.

Del Aziz gives us a crooked smile in return. 'And may the night bring us all luminous dreams, as they say up in the Citadel.'

150

CHAPTER NINETEEN

The City of Dreams

As night turns to day and the miles clock down towards Mumbai, the houses – a mix of shacks and larger buildings – become more numerous and more substantial, some of them rising many floors into the sky, casting shadows across our path. My breathing comes easier as our little cart becomes one of many, the three of us concealed in the throng of people, all like worker ants scuttling to our various destinations across the city.

We turn down a small side street and Amir slows his cart. 'Let us say goodbye here,' he says, 'where it is quiet. I wish you all the best, Mimi Malou. You have a difficult path ahead and many lives to save.'

My mouth feels dry at the thought of my parents

151

waiting to be sentenced, and the king dying of nightmares.

Rafi coughs awkwardly as we unload our bags from Amir's cart. 'Can I ask you what happened to your dream creature when you left the Citadel? I don't know what I'd do without Mithi.'

Amir sighs. 'Delilah would have been overwhelmed by the volume of dreams on offer in the outer world, so I left her back home in the Citadel. Such a beautiful creature, an oriental dwarf kingfisher. Madame Noori will pass her on to a suitable student in time, I'm sure.'

'That must have been hard, to leave your creature and not have her when you sleep,' I say.

'The ache softens eventually. It never goes away completely, but that's okay. The memory is too beautiful to lose.' Amir's eyes are a little shiny. 'Anyway, Mimi and Rafi, this is where we part. It was a pleasure to meet you both,' he says, quickly changing the subject. 'May you have luminous thoughts.'

'Thank you, Amir. And may your dreams shine ever brightly,' I reply.

The sounds and colours of Mumbai are more vibrant than any dream I have ever seen. We wander along the streets watching people shouting, bargaining, arguing,

152

calling. The air is filled with the delicious spicy scent of street food and simmering pots of chai, and I have never felt so alive and yet so alone. We weave through the stalls and crowds of strangers, doing our best to stay unseen.

'Where do your friends live?' I ask. My feet are beginning to ache with the walking, and I am losing any sense of direction I had.

'They shift their camp from time to time,' says Rafi. 'It's not like they have a fancy apartment. It's just a tent and a bunch of kids who look after each other.'

'It sounds hard,' I say, thinking of my comfortable bedroom in our apartment above the library. I have never needed to worry about keeping warm or what my next meal will be. 'But if they're going to help us,' I say, 'how shall we know where to find them?'

'We'll find each other soon enough,' he says. 'They probably know we're here already.'

Clouds of dust hit the back of my throat as we cross a busy road. Lalu flutters ahead of us, excited by all the people and the dreams that might be caught. Mithi seems a little scared in comparison and Rafi holds her close. I worry about Amir's parting words. Leaving his dream creature at home to keep her safe . . . With luck,

Rafi and I will bring our creatures safely back to the Citadel very soon.

As we walk along, the crowd becomes a thicket of elbows and bags. I am pushed off the pavement into the gutter along the road. Rafi and I cross to the other side of the street and find ourselves rubbing our empty tummies outside a bakery with a dazzling display of cakes and bread. Hunger draws us inside. The shopkeeper looks up and casts a lazy eye over us.

'You two are dressed too well for street kids,' he says and scratches his chin as he leans across the counter.

Behind him the shelves are crammed with crusty loaves and in the glass counter at the front are rows of fresh cream cakes and little cinnamon rolls. Rafi points to a piece of chocolate cake and I to a strawberry eclair.

'That'll be one hundred rupees,' says the man, holding out his hand.

Rafi stares at him in disbelief. 'You must be joking! Are they filled with solid gold?'

I shush him and take out my purse. 'Is this okay?' My mind is trembling as much as my hand. The silver coin is probably worth more than all the cakes in the shop, but we don't have much choice until we get some local money.

The man holds the coin in his lobster-like pincer grip and pulls his glasses down a little, peering at the inscriptions. He's silent for a moment, then a slow smile cracks open on his moon-like face and he wipes his long moustache, nodding slowly. I reach for our package with hungry, sweaty hands—

'Hey! Bring that back!' The shopkeeper has suddenly looked up to the entrance, where another boy has just left the shop, a loaf of bread under his arm. 'Are you two working with them? Thieves!' he shouts. 'Get out of here!'

'You have my money!' I say, but the baker rises up, face taut as he shoos us out.

'Thieves, scoundrels! Get out!'

We back away, terrified that the hullabaloo will usher in some unwanted attention. Rafi stumbles out of the door, and I follow. I run, trying to keep an eye on Rafi, but my mind is racing, the man's voice ringing in my head. I keep going, heart pounding and legs on fire. I don't stop until the echoing shouts of the shopkeeper have been washed away by the crowds and carts around me.

'That was close,' I shout, but there is no reply. I slow down and look around, but Rafi is nowhere to be seen and I am swimming in a sea of strangers, filled with an ice-cold awareness that I am alone and helpless.

A man leaning on a pillar across the street chews on a pencil and casts a lazy eye in my direction. Could he be a spy working with my aunt or the crown prince? Another man on the back of a cart slows down and shouts something at me, but I don't understand him, so I pull my bag close and walk along briskly. Rafi's friends might be looking for him, but who will look for me?

I decide I need to find the station because Rafi might have gone there, but I feel as helpless as a piece of seaweed going with the ebb and flow of the tide. I skirt past bags and elbows, watching shoppers haggling for supplies. It feels like the dance of words between seller and buyer is part of a ritual here. In a different time, I would enjoy learning to play the game, but for now I feel heavy with despair. How will I stop the king being killed if I cannot even find my way out of Mumbai?

I duck into a dark, narrow gap between two buildings and will myself not to cry.

'Come on, Lalu,' I whisper as she pokes her head out of the soft nest in my pocket, 'we still have each other,' and I take a few deep breaths to calm myself. But as I peep back out into the street, I hear the crunch of footsteps behind me and a discarded can rolls past my shoe.

'Nice bag you have there,' says a man's rough voice.

I pull my bag closer and slowly turn to face him. He has two missing teeth and gives me a crooked smile as he reaches out to seize my belongings.

'No, it's mine!' I splay my fingers and poke the man in his eye.

The would-be thief howls and doubles over, then with one eye still covered he reaches out, swiping his arms towards my bag. Lalu zooms towards his head and pokes her long beak at his ears.

He pauses in wonder as her dream threads light up the shadows with a soft, comforting glow and sink onto his head, but the dream fades quickly and he shakes himself, a new hunger etched on his face.

'I've heard of them dream birds. Magic like that is worth something – let me at it!'

A bright blue blur, Lalu flits beyond his reach and back into my hands as we scarper out of the alleyway and plunge back into the crowd.

After a few minutes of shuffling along, I notice

someone walking beside me, a boy, about my height, with messy, dusty hair. I think of Rafi, but this boy seems older and even more street smart. I look around for somewhere to escape to if he tries to grab my bag.

'You're new here, aren't you?' he whispers. I want to believe he means no harm, but harm has made a point of coming at me again and again so far today.

I lift my chin and pout, trying not to let him see I'm scared, but he laughs.

'It's okay. You look like you could do with some friends.' He pats me on the shoulder. 'Come with me.'

Fear and curiosity prick me like tiny ants crawling down the back of my neck. I narrow my eyes. I miss being able to rely on people to be good.

'Don't worry, you can trust me. I'm a friend of a friend,' he says. 'Been hearing all about you. Hungry?'

I look away, though my stomach churns at the idea of some food.

'Cat got your tongue?' he asks.

'No, but I don't talk to strangers.'

'Ah. She speaks.' He smiles. 'My name is Kantar.' He pulls a bag of sweet doughnuts out from his pocket and offers me one.

'Thank you, but no.' My mouth is watering but I

don't want to put myself in debt to someone I've only just met.

'It's okay. It isn't poisoned or anything.' He points behind me. 'Eat it before he does!'

I turn, and who do I see but Rafi running towards me, and Mithi too, bobbing over the crowds excitedly.

'Rafi!' I cry. 'I lost you!'

'The shopkeeper caught up with me,' says Rafi. 'The old crook tried to get some more coins. Luckily, Kantar and his friends distracted him and we managed to get away. *With doughnuts*. We're okay now, Mimi. I've known this scoundrel longer than I can remember.'

'Friends stay strong,' says Kantar, handing out doughnuts to a small group of children in various states of scruffiness.

'Through right and wrong!' says Rafi, clapping his friend on the back.

'Now, eat,' says Kantar, thrusting the last doughnut into my hands. I take a small bite. It's soft and warm and filled with a syrupy-sweet raspberry jam, and I finish the rest of it in three mouthfuls, wiping the sugary crumbs from my face.

I tell Kantar and the others the whole story: about the Citadel, and the king of Ratnagar suffering nightmares that no one can stop, about my parents being unjustly blamed and held for treason, and my aunt turning dreams into nightmares.

Kantar shakes his head. 'Plenty of us have terrible relatives, but this is next-level bad.'

'It is. Everyone thinks my parents are traitors and poisoners, but it's a lie. If the king dies, my parents will never be free, and my aunt will start to sell nightmares again. She's already having them moved to Ratnagar.'

'Ratnagar is very far away,' says Kantar. 'We can take you to the station tomorrow. Stay with us tonight – it'll be safer than on the streets.'

I shake my head. 'We don't have time. If there is a night train, we need to get it.'

A girl steps forward. She is taller than me and has striking green eyes that pierce me with a quizzical look and my face reddens. 'Why is everyone so bothered about Ratnagar?' she says. 'And what can *you* do to help when you get there? You're just one girl!'

'This is my friend Zaini,' says Rafi, 'ever the pessimist.'

'Realist.' Zaini pouts.

I give Zaini a smile. It's not immediately returned but she throws me a small nod.

'Ratnagar is the main trading post in the Northern

Kingdoms,' I explain. 'In the past, our people used it as a marketplace to find new customers, but then some of the dream threaders became greedy and started to create nightmare potions.'

'Bad enough to control someone, Zaini, or even kill them,' adds Rafi.

Zaini's eyes darken. 'Why would they do that?'

'Plenty of folk would pay a lot of money for that kind of power. When King Ganipal found out, he banned his kingdom from working with our dream threaders. He closed the sale of any dream threading, good or evil.'

'So why is Ratnagar important to you now?' asks Zaini. Her eyes widen as she watches Lalu settling on the floor beside my bag. 'Does their king rule your Citadel too?'

I shake my head. 'We are ruled by no one. The head librarian oversees the Citadel council, but we have no king or queen. Ratnagar is a place we traded with until the king shut everything down. Rogue dream threaders selling nightmares caused trouble for us all, so my parents visited Ratnagar. They wanted to bring the Citadel and Ratnagar close again, but people said they were trying to blackmail the king – but that was a lie.

They were set up, betrayed by my aunt and the king's own son, Crown Prince Sakim, who are trying to re-create the market for nightmares. And for that they need to get rid of the man blocking it.'

Zaini scrunches her nose. 'Yes, yes, but I'll ask my question again: what are *you* going to do about it? What good will *you* be? How will you fight against a prince, even if what you say is true?'

My hands prickle with anger, and I clench them to stop them striking out at her. Though her words sting, there is truth in what she says.

'I won't give up, Zaini, you can be sure of that. I've already got this far. I will find a way to Ratnagar, because if I don't prove my parents' innocence and prevent the king's murder, everything I love about the Citadel will be lost for ever.'

Rafi rubs his eyes. 'I'm going with Mimi,' he says. 'I've got to see this one through. Will you come with us? There's power in numbers.'

Zaini fixes him with an eagle eye. 'We can't risk our lives for a stranger. Look around . . . all these little kids. My brother's one of them.'

'You all do what you need to,' says Rafi, 'but I'm going.'

162

'I can't promise riches,' I say, 'but when the Citadel is restored, it will once again be free to welcome those in need. If you need a home, we will find one for you there.'

Kantar clears his throat. 'I want to grow old here in Mumbai, but I want a house with proper walls and a roof, and a bathroom where I can wash without—'

'Where you can go to the toilet in peace, eh? I just remembered how long you take in the mornings . . .' Rafi laughs as Kantar pinches his arm.

'Well, I suppose if the price is right, it could give us the money to find somewhere we can call home,' says Zaini with a half-smile, and with that we are agreed. Rafi and I will carry on to Ratnagar, and Kantar and Zaini will join us.

Kantar sends the other kids back to camp with a promise he and Zaini will return in a matter of days and dispenses a few coins in each of their palms. Then, after we've walked along a couple more streets and turned a couple more corners, we are suddenly at Mumbai Central train station, and the four of us follow the tide of travellers into its cavernous entrance.

I wonder if my parents took this journey, aware of the dangers they were walking into.

I hope I don't repeat their mistakes.

CHAPTER TWENTY

The Bird Hunt

I push down a bubble of fear as the grinding, clattering station opens its mouth. Up until leaving the Citadel yesterday, I have never been anywhere I couldn't walk to. The trains inside Mumbai Central seem to go on for ever. All different colours, and so long and wide it takes my breath away that so many people exist, let alone so many destinations. Travellers criss-cross their way across the platforms, dragging bags, boxes and families, as the trains screech and puff steam, urging them on board and whistling as they leave.

There is a seating area in the middle of the station, where grubby metal benches are filled with travellers and their bags. I scan across it but there is no space for the four of us, so we huddle close in a corner between a snack stand and a newsagent's.

A grumpy policeman approaches us, pulling up his trousers by his belt and taking out a notepad. He shows us his badge: *Officer J. Todiwala.*

'What are all you kids doing here?' He crosses his arms as he looks us up and down. 'You're trouble. I can smell it.'

Kantar lifts his arms and sniffs his armpits and we simmer with laughter, but the policeman's face creases in anger and he yanks on Kantar's collar.

'You think you're some kind of clown, eh? No begging in the station.'

Rafi clears his throat. 'We're not begging, sir, we are here to—'

'Tickets?' he grunts. 'Where are your tickets?'

'Please, sir, we are waiting for my parents,' I say. 'They are arriving from Ratnagar, via Delhi.'

The policeman purses his lips and shakes his head. 'Which train?'

I glance at the arrivals board and pick one of the later trains.

'That one, the 21:30 train from Delhi. In two hours. They told us to wait here, Officer. They are learned

165

scholars and have been to Ratnagar of the Northern Kingdoms to do some work for the king.'

'King Ganipal of Ratnagar? My, my, what a strange tale. Poor old fellow. I heard he is most unwell.' He scratches his head. 'Okay, you can stay here, but any trouble and you'll be seeing the back of my police van. It's waiting outside . . .'

I gulp.

He turns to look at us and frowns, then turns his attention to the waft of sweet spiced chai from the snack stand behind us.

The speakers fizzle and crackle and the stationmaster's voice booms across the station: '*Last call for the 19:45 Great Northern Express to Ratnagar, calling at Ravindabad, Madhapura and Delhi. Departing from platform six in ten minutes.*'

'Okay, platform six! We just have to run,' I say. 'Let's split into two groups and head to the train.'

'Good plan,' says Zaini. 'We'll meet in the third-class carriage. Mimi, I'll go with you; Kantar and Rafi, we'll see you on the train.'

We all put our thumbs up – but then I hear a familiar sound:

Click, clack.

I wipe a sheen of sweat from my brow; my courage slumps away.

Click, clack.

I shrink into the corner and pull my bag close to my chest. My plans are crumbling, like a castle in the sand.

Aunt Moyna is here, in Mumbai, and it looks like she has brought two dream technicians with her. Her trolley rattles and rumbles across the station. It sounds like it contains glass bottles. Could it be dreams or, worse still, nightmares? She pauses to look at the departure board.

'I need to hide,' I whisper to Zaini.

She wrinkles her forehead. 'Hurry, Mimi! We need to get to the train. That way.'

But 'that way' means sneaking past my aunt and, ticketless, onto the train?

I can barely form the words, but grip Zaini's arm. 'She's here! My aunt!'

'I'll walk in front and cause a distraction,' she says, but I shake my head.

'Better to stay hidden.' I pull my hood over my head, but Lalu is fluttering above the heads of the waiting passengers slumped on benches as she searches for sleepers with dreams to spare. I hold out my hand and she spots me, darting in my direction with her belly full of threads, but too late I realize that in the grey world of the station a bright blue hummingbird can be a dangerous distraction. People look up and point.

'Come on,' I whisper, but my breath gives way to ice. Sitting on a metal beam under the roof of the station is a dark-feathered bird with dangerous red eyes. Eyes that are locked on Lalu.

It is Kala. I think of the danger Lalu is in, her tiny hummingbird frame no match for an angry koel.

'Come on, Lalu!' I shout.

Kala tucks his wings back and zips towards her with frightening speed.

Rafi is tugging my sleeve but his words, urgent and anxious, seem far away.

'Hurry, Lalu!' but even Mithi cannot help my dream creature now. Rafi's chiffchaff flits in and out, trying to distract Kala, but it's futile. Lalu's tiny body only has so much energy, and Kala gains on her, circling her so she's frightened and confused. Two ravens caw with pleasure as they join in the hunt.

Rafi and the others throw stones at the larger birds, but they swivel up and down, the three of them homing in on Lalu. I reach towards her, but just as she is in fingers' reach, she's knocked by a raven and falls to the ground, her store of dreams falling out of her, scattering over unsuspecting travellers below. I race over and pick her up. Though her tiny chest is still fluttering, her eyes are shut.

I can hear my aunt calling my name, but I no longer care.

Lalu is broken.

CHAPTER TWENTY-ONE

A Close Call

Officer Todiwala has finished his chai, but the kerfuffle brings him running towards us.

'Sir, I must ask you to help us.' Zaini presses her hands together, eyes wide, as she tells a frightful lie. 'That lady –' she points to Aunt Moyna click-clacking towards us across the station concourse – 'she is trying to kidnap my friend here.'

The officer scratches his chin. '*Whaaaat?* While you all wait for her kind parents who are helping King Ganipal?' He strides off towards my aunt and the two technicians accompanying her.

Zaini shakes my arm.

'Come on, Mimi. That's taken care of her. We need to go.'

'Can't. Lalu. Look.' My feet are welded to the ground and my words can barely form themselves. My dream creature lies limp in my hands, her breath shallow.

'You said the only way to save your parents is to save the king.' She puts an arm around my shoulder. 'We need to get on the train, or we'll be too late.'

I lower Lalu into the nest of leaves in my pocket.

Aunt Moyna's shrill protestations drift over to us as Officer Todiwala challenges her.

'This is all a silly misunderstanding, Officer. The girl is my niece. My late brother's daughter.' She points to her chin then towards mine. 'Don't you see the family resemblance?'

Her 'late' brother? Her deceit whips up a deep anger inside me and I erupt. 'She is lying!' I shout.

Aunt Moyna's face is a picture of confusion. Eyes askew, mouth open, she realizes I am not the quiet mouse she knew in the Citadel.

Officer Todiwala trills on his whistle, bringing a surge of police officers into the station. My aunt's hands fly in all directions, and she point towards us, but Officer Todiwala is having none of it. He demands she open

171

her suitcase, and she's shaking her head and shouting towards us. We waste no time and scarper towards platform six.

'Stop her!' Aunt Moyna yells.

Officer Todiwala grabs her, but she breaks away, running toward me; Kala is hot on her heels and filled with menacing green dream threads.

Zaini and I leap onto the nearest train and crouch down, running the length of the carriage. Then we sneak out on the rail side and climb onto the adjacent train. We run across this one, and the next, until we reach platform six, where the Great Northern Express is preparing to leave.

Shrill whistles and shouting break out above the general hubbub of noise and I spy Todiwala and some of his fellow officers pursuing my aunt. We race along the platform.

'How much further?' I shout, as we catch up with Rafi and Kantar.

'We need to get to the end,' shouts Rafi.

'Unreserved seats,' cries Kantar.

As I fall back behind my friends, Kantar reaches out his hand and pulls me forward. I feel a surge of hope as, behind me, the whistles stop and I hear my aunt shouting at Officer Todiwala. I sneak a look across the platform and see her being held back by the policeman.

'Let – me – go!'

At the other end of the platform, I see Zaini struggling against one of my aunt's technicians.

Another whistle now, loud and insistent. The engine driver blows the horn as the intercity express prepares to leave. The stationmaster's voice comes again over the tannoy, warning passengers to climb aboard.

The smell of diesel fills the air as the engines start to chug.

Kantar jumps on first, holding the door open and pulling Rafi onto the train.

I'm still on the platform and point back at Zaini, who is arguing with the man. 'She's in trouble!' I shout.

The man is whispering to Zaini, and she goes still for a moment as if she is listening. Then she wriggles and kicks his shin. He lets go of her and hops around in pain, leaving her free to run towards me.

The train starts to chug. I wait a moment for Zaini to catch up. The technician holds back, and I notice he has a suspicious smile on his face.

Why is he not chasing us?

My aunt is still arguing with the police officers, and they bundle her away.

Zaini sprints so fast she's soon run past me, and she leaps onto the train as it moves out, sinking at Rafi and Kantar's feet, heaving to catch her breath – but I am caught by surprise and suddenly realize I am alone on the platform. I start to run again, but my momentum is weak and the train gathers pace.

Rafi reaches down for me, hanging onto a door with one hand and stretching his other arm towards me. 'Hold onto my hand!'

His voice is blown away as the train edges further away, pulling my friends away from me.

Carriage after carriage start to pass; my friends run back through the moving train shouting at me to keep going.

Kantar pops his head out of a window. 'Mimi! Just grab something!'

I look to my left and fling my arm out, grabbing a bar on one side of a carriage door, and I pray as I pull myself up and lean in as close as I can. I breathe out and make myself as flat as I possibly can, feeling the rush of air over me as darkness fills the air and we enter a tunnel.

I hold my head close to the train. My bag pummels along the wall, knocking the breath out of me, but I hold firm, eyes squeezed closed, knowing my life is hanging by a gossamer thread.

Then suddenly the tunnel ends and I am bathed in moonlight. I lift my head and look around. By now the train is careering along through the slums of Mumbai and I'm overwhelmed by the noise and the smell of hundreds of rickety shacks clustered along the railway line. I reach out to the handle of the door and carefully twist the handle.

My hands, slick with sweat, struggle to hold me steady as I inch towards the carriage door. I need to pull myself through and it takes every drop of energy to pull the door away a little. It catches a gust of wind and flies open. I hear a woman scream and an arm reaches out to close it, but when she sees me she screams again.

'Are you mad?' she cries.

'Help me . . . *please!*' I start to slide as I lose my grip.

The woman calls someone else, a thin, bearded man who holds his arm out towards me. I'm too scared to let go of the rail but he grabs hold of my wrists and pulls me into the carriage. I land with a thud on the floor of the train and a crowd of passengers forms around me.

I'm safe.

CHAPTER TWENTY-TWO

The Great Northern Express

I pull myself up and half stumble, half crawl towards the unreserved carriage, where I find the others huddled on a wooden bench. I slump to the floor near the window as Rafi gives me a gigantic hug.

Gingerly, I scoop Lalu out of her pocket nest. She is lying very still and the flash of gold feathers on the nape of her neck is fading. Mithi perches close by, but she has only a few scattered dream threads and these won't be enough to save Lalu. Then I remember . . . *I can save her with magic!* I tear open my bag and fish out the brown-leather book from the library. Lalu has gifted me her dream threads so many times, and I must return the favour.

My hand shakes as I hold my dream hook in one hand and flick through the book with the other. Rafi looks over my shoulder and stops me when we reach the dream he knows too well. In the dream laboratory, Aunt Moyna and her dream technicians used dream magic to extract dreams from Rafi and from others before him. Dreams taken before they had even been forgotten. A freshly captured dream is potent. It could revive Lalu.

The Spell of Dream Extraction

A spell to remove dreams before they are forgotten.*
Hold the dream hook to the space
between the dreamer's eyes.
Twist the hook three times clockwise and four times
counterclockwise as the magician recites the following spell:

I call the thread towards the light,
My hook will firmly hold its bite.
No more will nightmares cast a shawl!
May minds be free of worries all!

* Warning – not to be used without permission
or only in case of extreme nightmares.

I close my eyes and slow my breathing. I picture the mountains above the Citadel. In June, streams cascade from their peaks, watering the soft, cushiony grass. I pull my mind back to a trip with my parents into the forest. My mother had packed warm samosas and syrupy sweets with a flask of chai for us to feast on. We spent the day spotting dream creatures in the wild, classifying them and trying to guess which human in the Citadel they would choose.

As I sink into the memory, I hold my dream hook close to my head. The feel the metal hook warm up as it senses the thread of the memory and catches it. Like a dream, it slips out of my mind and the image starts to fade until it turns to darkness in my mind. I open my eyes to find a magnificent thread coiled around the hook. Golden, helical, sparkling. It glitters as I gently coax the full length of it onto my hook and bring it away from my head.

'It's beautiful,' gasps Zaini, 'like a jewelled necklace.'

'It's a grade one dream thread,' says Rafi, 'freshly pressed.'

This time, it's me who is nervous of losing the dream. Carefully, I unravel the dream thread over Lalu. It melts into her, coating her in a golden glow. She shivers a moment then her breath softens and, as the dream fades, Lalu opens her eyes. I whisper soft encouragement as her energy returns.

'She's better!' Zaini beams and reaches a tender finger out to stroke Lalu's neck. 'Such a beautiful creature.'

'Yes, the thread seems to have revived her,' I whisper, grateful for the kinder words than I'm used to from Zaini.

Mithi coos in approval and watches over Lalu as we plan the next part of our journey.

The crowds shift and squirm in the steaming-hot carriage, as travellers and vendors pass through. Luckily, our tiny corner is next to a window, and I pull the glass down to let in some fresh air.

My eye is caught by something in Zaini's hand. She is clutching a feather. It's plain black, but something about it feels different, and I feel a surge of nausea when her hand shifts and in the light of the carriage the feather shimmers softly.

'Where did you find that?'

She looks at it as if surprised then turns her gaze to me. 'I found it on the floor. I like the way it feels.'

'It shimmers because it has held dreams . . . it comes from a dream creature – Zaini, where did you find it?'

I feel prickles of fear running over my skin. My heart quickens. If there is a dream creature on the train, there could be one of my aunt's dream technicians.

Zaini throws the black feather out of the train window. 'Just forget about it. I found it on the platform at Mumbai. I didn't realize it was anything special.'

'It was probably from when that technician was chasing us,' says Kantar.

Rafi shakes his head and looks out of the window, as if he wants to keep an eye on the feather, but it is long gone.

Rickety slick.

Rickety slick.

And so the train chugs on.

*

As we approach another city, the dusty, sandy towns are replaced by shacks and ramshackle buildings that hug each other like long-forgotten family. The train screeches as it slides into the station.

'Keep hold of your seat, Mimi,' says Rafi as the carriage erupts into chaotic activity: a rush of people standing, pulling bags off racks and a slow march to the doors. As they swing open, my senses are assaulted by a chorus of noise and colour, and the smell of freshly

180

cooked food. Vendors walk along the platform pushing paper cones stuffed with peanuts and pakoras into grateful hands stretched through the open windows along the train. My stomach rumbles. We didn't have time to eat in the station. Between people pushing their way off the train and others barging on, we hold on tight to the wooden benches we are seated on, then Rafi extracts himself and leans out of the window, catches a trader's eye, and barters a little for a packet of pakoras and a couple of bottles of soda.

As we scoff our food down, the ticket inspector appears in our carriage. He is not much older or taller than Kantar but has a small sprout of hair above his lip and an officious air. His hair is carefully greased and combed, and he taps his badge as he approaches us.

'Where did you board?' he asks us.

'Just now, sir. We are going to Delhi.' The rest of us keep our faces poker straight at Kantar's lie.

The man nods and pulls his cap back. Then he turns his head and looks straight at me.

'You look familiar,' he says. I feel my neck go cold as he puts his hands on his hips and stares at me for a moment. I look him in the eye. I don't want to make him think I'm hiding anything.

The inspector shakes his head, shrugs his shoulders and turns his attention to his ticket machine as I hand over the money for our journey. We are left with a few small coins.

'We'll need to think of a way to get more money,' I say when the inspector has moved on. 'This won't be enough.'

Kantar pats my shoulder. 'Don't worry, Mimi, that is something we can do.'

'No stealing,' I say, wagging my finger at them and trying out my most severe frown, but it seems to have the wrong effect as they fall about laughing.

'I can tell you never had a brother or sister to threaten,' says Kantar.

'No. My aunt used to have a cat called Frou-Frou and I tried it out on her, but strangely enough it never worked.'

'Frou-Frou?' cackles Zaini. 'A name like that makes me think she must have been a very pampered cat indeed!'

'She was. Prime fish from the river market in Songra, and a plate of whatever we ate for dinner. She was a sweet thing really, but she had a taste for hunting the dream creatures. My mother's bluebird came to a

182

painful end, and Frou-Frou was sent to a school in Songra.'

The four of us lie across the seats and the floor as the train rattles on into the inky night on its way north.

'Zaini,' I whisper, 'would you like a dream creature one day?'

'I don't know,' she says. 'I have to take care of my brother and that's more than enough for me to worry about.'

'Perhaps, when all this is done, we can visit each other though.' My tummy turns a little. I have never had many friends and it would be nice if Rafi's friends became my friends too.

'Of course we will,' she says. 'Friends stay strong . . .'

'Through right and wrong,' I whisper, and a soft smile lets itself grow inside me.

CHAPTER TWENTY-THREE

Ticket troubles

The gentle rhythm of the train speeding over the track lulls us into dreamland and, when we stretch awake, we find ourselves steaming into the Delhi metropolis. From here, the line starts to head into the mountains, so most of the travellers get off, leaving a few farmers and families with screeching children who are so tired they cannot sleep.

The changeover brings a welcome lull to the crowds and chaos of the last twenty hours. We spread our belongings out on the upper and lower benches at one end of the unreserved carriage.

I leaf through the book of dream magic to find a spell to reach my parents. They are deep in the dungeons under the palace of Ratnagar, with many layers of guards to get past . . .

My thoughts are interrupted by the scent of spiced potatoes and fried puris coming through the open window in the door leading to the next carriage. A food vendor is making her way down the train. My stomach rumbles in grateful anticipation but, as I poke my head out into the aisle, I see someone behind her who makes me pull back into the shadows, as if gripped in a vice so tight I can barely breathe. The others look at me with confused concern.

'Suri.'

I can only manage a whisper but it's enough to cause Rafi's face to drain of colour.

The woman behind the food vendor is wearing a cornflower-blue silk suit. She slopes towards us along the aisle of the carriage in front, peering up and down into the corners of all the passenger booths. Anyone else watching her might wonder for a moment why such a smartly dressed lady would be taking such an interest in an unreserved carriage of a train chugging its way up into the far north, but beyond this casual curiosity they would soon forget her. Not so with us, however. This woman's hair is dark black with a streak of white, and sitting on her shoulder is a raven whose belly glints with malicious red and green threads of nightmares and evil dreams.

There are several groups of people clustered around the entrance to our carriage, and the food vendor is moving ahead of her very slowly, so Suri hasn't spotted us yet, but it is just a matter of time.

'Suri?' questions Kantar. 'Who's she?'

'One of the meanest and baddest dream technicians from the Citadel,' Rafi explains. 'We need to hide.'

Kantar tuts and casts a glance towards the dream technician. 'No way! I haven't even had breakfast and we've got to deal with more funny business.'

Zaini furrows her brow. 'Weren't the Citadel folk taken away by Officer Todiwala in Mumbai?'

'We didn't see the end of it all, and we never saw *her*. Maybe Suri managed to avoid the police. Maybe she used the distraction to sneak onto the train,' I whisper.

Suri pauses a minute as the ticket collector starts making his checks. Rafi and I place protective hands around Mithi and Lalu as the raven squawks angrily. Carab must have sensed us, but Suri is too busy poking her nose into the top and bottom benches to notice.

The guard blows the whistle. My heart quickens as Suri beckons Carab and tries to push past the food vendor, but she is blocked by Kantar who is striding along the aisle in her direction. He looks back and winks then trips over as he nears her, bumping into her shoulder.

Suri brushes her shoulder, her face creased in disgust. 'Watch where you step, you filthy rat.'

Kantar bows and mutters profuse apologies. He fakes an oily humility very well, and we silently cheer him on as we notice him dipping his hand into Suri's jacket pocket as he passes. When he reaches the other end of the carriage, he looks back and gives us a quick smile, flashing Suri's ticket in his hand. As much as I disapprove of stealing, on this occasion I am filled with gratitude.

The tannoy announces the train's imminent departure and the ticket collector approaches Suri to check her ticket, but her hand is as empty as her pocket and she screams, looking around with bulging eyes, screaming of theft and young urchins. Distracted by her confusion and anger, she fails to notice me and Rafi watching, with smiles across our faces as the ticket inspector harries her to the door.

'No, no, you must go to the ticket office on the

platform.' The man ignores Suri's protestations, her repeated 'Do you know who I am?' and hustles her off the train with surprising strength of mind and hand gestures. It is no small effort to hold back our yelps of joy until after the engines start to chug, pulling us away from Suri, scowling and scarlet-faced, on the platform in Delhi station.

Kantar finds his way back with nimble-footed speed, poking his head out of the window to give us a running commentary. 'Ha! She's stamping her foot now . . . Now she's wagging her finger at a porter . . . Ho! Look at her arguing!'

We laugh and settle back onto our benches with a lightness of spirit I haven't felt in days. Very soon the tenements and houses at the edge of Delhi give way to rocky outcrops and rising hills as we continue north towards the mountain kingdom of Ratnagar. This part of the journey is slower, as the train trundles over the winding track.

'Mimi, tell us about your parents – what are they like?' asks Zaini.

The question sends my mind into a whirlwind. For the past two years, my aunt's lies have seeded anger and disappointment in me whenever I've thought of my parents. Yet they are innocent. They've tried to reach out to me and reassure me.

'They are loving, and they are strong,' I say, 'though I am worried I am beginning to forget them.'

If my plan works out, I will see them soon and together we will bring justice to the king, to Ratnagar and to our Citadel.

The train starts to slow as the track ahead rises and circles ever upward into the mountains, and I feel goose pimples on my arms. The sky outside is bright blue and cloudless, but soon we can see our breath steaming and we shut the window to try and keep out the cold air. The trees become stumpy, bushy and sparse and the villages we pass are just rocky outposts, a world away from the noise and light of the big cities we have travelled through.

The ticket collector does another round after we pick up a few farmers from a provincial railway station at the beginning of the Northern Kingdoms and this time, we are caught in his scan of passengers. 'You told me you were getting off at Delhi. For Ratnagar, there is a supplement.' He holds his hand out and stares at each of us in turn.

'We already paid in Delhi,' says Zaini.

The man frowns. 'Tickets.'

I look to Lalu to help us find a dreamy escape. She and Mithi have had a night of hunting and they are full of glorious threads. They fly like sprites under the roof of the carriage and, as the man looks up, a shower of gold, orange and silver falls over him. Bright specks shaped like snowflakes, stars and tiny glistening spheres spin in different directions and settle over him. A gleaming smile spreads across the ticket collector's face as he sinks into a beautiful dream. My friends cheer in whispers. Quickly and gently, we settle him into a seat in the next carriage, putting Suri's ticket in his hand. We pull his hat over his eyes and he starts to snore gently.

'Ah, a good sleeper,' says Kantar, and we run back to our carriage, giggling like a flock of parrots. I glow with pride as I realize how well I have learned to hide and sneak like the best of street kids.

Rafi and I tuck our dream creatures back in our pockets and plan our next move. On the side of the windows, signs of a mountain kingdom start to appear: schools, shops, houses and – odd among the gilded buildings – an old factory that seems abandoned.

Ratnagar is closing in.

CHAPTER TWENTY-FOUR

Unwelcome News

An ornate clock face adorns the entrance to the Ratnagar city hall. Its golden hands glint in the bright morning sunlight as the bell chimes eight times. We lurk close to the gateway of this grand, five-storeyed building and look over the main square. Hawkers and traders are setting up scattered stalls as the city folk start to go about their day.

Two women pass us on their way into the city hall. One has a newspaper under her arm which she drops into a rubbish bin as she enters the building. I see a picture of the king on the front, so I scoot over and grab it. It's a copy of the *Ratnagar Star*, and the headline story sends a chill down my spine.

KING GANIPAL SERIOUSLY UNWELL

Crown Prince to chair
Council of Elders meeting.

From our Royal Correspondent, Asha Hamied.

The king's health took a turn for the worse late on Wednesday night and the extended Royal Family has gathered to spend what could be his final days with him. As the king becomes more detached from everyday life, tests remain inconclusive and concerns are mounting over his chances of making a full recovery.

Despite his decline, doctors continue to urge active care amid reports of a disagreement between the royal physician and Crown Prince Sakim. Dr Sonny Balbul has requested the king be transferred to a specialist unit at the Royal Prestige Hospital in Delhi. Friends of the prince, however, say he does not want his father to be moved in such a delicate state. The prince is said to be personally tending to the king's health in a mark of profound filial tenderness.

An emergency meeting of the Council of Elders has been convened for tomorrow morning to arrange a temporary transfer of power to the crown prince. We understand the long-awaited Royal Jubilee Ball to celebrate the king's silver jubilee will go ahead as planned this evening. A large number of distinguished guests are expected to arrive in Ratnagar today for this momentous and possibly final occasion to celebrate our much-loved monarch.

'Oh,' I gasp, 'the council meeting has been moved to tomorrow.' I pull out the letters from my parents I found in my aunt's office drawer. 'They said they would be judged at the next meeting. And it sounds like it's been brought forward because of the king being so ill.'

Zaini puts her arm round me. 'Then there is no time to lose.'

I stiffen as trumpets sound and horses ridden by red-coated soldiers canter past. People stop and stare. A young boy carrying a toy cart drops it as his mother pulls him away from the road. His cries go unheeded in the noise and disturbance, but I manage to pluck the toy out of the way before the rush of hooves can crush it. The boy wipes his nose and holds out his snotty hands for a hug as I return his cart. His mother remains oblivious, her attention focused on the passing troops.

'I wonder if the king's still alive,' says an old woman behind us.

'If the red-cloaks are riding, it means the prince is taking control,' says the man next to her, who sways a little on his walking stick as one of the riders edges close by. 'Who knows what that means!'

'It means stability, my friends,' says another voice, one that sounds cold, harsh and strangely familiar. 'The prince is the rightful heir to Ratnagar. He has our best interests at heart.'

I shrink back as I look up and see the man addressing the old couple and the other citizens gathered around.

It's Jamal, but he doesn't notice me or my friends as he continues to make pronouncements on the dire state of the king's health. We slink away but my head is filled with a sharp collection of worries. If Jamal has arrived, then my aunt must surely be here too.

We search the city for somewhere to hide, a place Aunt Moyna wouldn't even think to look for us, and we find ourselves on a dirt track off a small street, well away from the centre of town. The Santana Lodge, a sandstone building, its doors and windows scruffy with peeling yellow paint, looks like a perfectly unremarkable place in which to tuck ourselves away.

The man at the reception desk asks no questions but gives us a key and shows us to our room. It has a cold stone floor and greasy yellow walls, with two sets of bunk beds lined up on each side and a desk by the window. He points out the small, shared bathroom at the end of the corridor.

As I wash away the dirt of the train journey, enjoying the feel of warm water on my skin and thinking about the dream I need to craft, Kantar raps on the bathroom door.

'Come on, Your Highness. When you're done in the bathroom, perhaps we can get some food?'

We find an inn nearby, and settle ourselves in clattery metal seats beside a wooden table. The owner, a kindly-looking man, brings us bowls of curry, rice and warm flatbreads while I tell the others my plan.

'I need to clear my parents' names and only the king can grant that, but if we want him to live, we need my mother and father's help. We have to find a way of getting them out of prison and into the royal quarters.'

Zaini clears her throat. 'How do we reach them?'

'We'll find a way,' says Kantar. 'I'll get chatting to people while you do your dream magic.'

Zaini groans. 'You and your chatting . . . he'll be there all day if we don't watch him.'

I bite my lip. 'I think I know a way to reach them. Something I read in the book of magic, but it's an advanced spell. If I work it right, though, we can use dream magic to control a person's behaviour. I've never heard of it being done in my lifetime, but the spell is in there, so it's worth a try.'

'Sounds dangerous,' says Rafi.

'It could be, but it is reversible. A dream will normally only last minutes. If we want to make it last longer, it has to be fashioned into a loop so it can run and run until it degrades. The book says we will have no more than an hour.'

I notice Zaini has written down my plan on a piece of paper which she covers when she sees me watching her.

'Sorry, I like to make lists. Keeps me focused,' she says, but her face flushes pink and she looks away.

Before we leave the inn, we sneak a glass bottle from our table into my bag. It'll serve to store the potion once it is ready to activate. Then Kantar and Zaini head to the palace to see what the security is like, while Rafi and I head back to the lodge. On our way there, we send Lalu and Mithi off hunting, telling them to find sleepers who might still be slumbering at this late hour of the morning.

We need threads. Lots of them. And we are running out of time.

CHAPTER TWENTY-FIVE

The Spell of Lucid Dreams

The spell I seek is at the back of the book, in a section for advanced practitioners, with dream magic to be done only after extensive training. I am not in the least qualified, but I have no choice. The security at the palace dungeons will be tight – there won't just be one or two guards to get past, but lots of them. We can maybe slink past some, maybe lie to others, but in somewhere as securely guarded as a palace dungeon, we'll need a little extra help.

When our dream creatures return, bellies glowing with threads of dreams from around Ratnagar, Rafi clears a space on the desk in our room and I place *The Magic of Dreams* down on it. Rafi removes the cap from the empty glass bottle, I find a cup in the bathroom and clean it out to use as a mixing bowl, then we take out our dream hooks.

The Spell of Lucid Dreams

A dark spell of mind control to be used for defensive purposes. All other uses are strictly prohibited.
The power of the spell will be diluted by the number of threads created. Only one dreamer is recommended per spell. With each additional dreamer, the spell will be halved in concentration, risking a loss of control or sudden awakening.

Equipment:
Dream threads – three per loop
Fragment of dream from the controller
Dream hooks.

Cast two dream threads into a loop. Add a thread from the mind of the controller.
Join the ends into a circle.*
Chant the following spell three times:

May this dream bring rest,
But may I confess
That while these threads shall turn and shake
My orders will the dreamer take.

* Warning – do not touch the thread, as the
dreamer must not sense the presence of the controller.

We decide to make five potions, hoping to use three at most. I use my hook to extract a live dream from myself as the controlling thread, unravelling it into the bowl. Rafi uses his hook to split it into five sections.

Using the threads that Lalu and Mithi have brought us, we join five pairs of threads together into twisted strands. Then we add one of my dream threads to each one and we weave and loop them into five circles. Once they are all done, I hold the hook over the cup and cast the spell. Then we drop the twisting, glittering dream loops into the bottle one by one ready to deploy over our targets. After securing the cap tightly on the bottle, I place it in the depths of my bag to hide it from sunlight.

When Kantar and Zaini return, we ask the lodge keeper for a sheet of paper so we can sketch out the palace.

'Everyone is thinking about the prince and the king, and about the ball this evening,' says Zaini, 'so now is as good a time as ever to get your parents out unnoticed.'

'Now is the *only* time,' I whisper. 'Tomorrow is their judgement day.'

On the floor beside my feet, I spot a feather. It is dark and stubby, and I recognize it as a raven's. Zaini kicks it away and squeezes my hand.

'We can do it,' she promises.

Kantar sketches out the off-road route he has uncovered leading to the dungeons at the back of the palace.

'There are two guards at the gate to the dungeon,' he says, 'and I heard from a man in town that they both have a sweet tooth.'

With a box of cakes from a local bakery (I don't ask Kantar how he got them), we take a circular route across town, veering off the main road onto a path that leads into the grasslands behind the palace.

'I think we should split up, Mimi. You and I are known to many hostile faces,' says Rafi.

Though it's hard to agree, I know he's right.

'I'll go with you, Mimi,' says Zaini.

We agree that Kantar and Rafi will keep watch, sending Mithi to signal to us if trouble is brewing. We split into pairs as we near the gate, Kantar and Rafi staying on the path while Zaini and I head in from the side.

There are two blue-cloaked guards at the gate, both around my father's age. Unlike Papa, they are bearded and wear black turbans. As Kantar and Rafi amble up the path towards them, the guards step forward, lances in hand, and block their way.

Kantar starts engaging the men in small talk. He is a skilful trickster, and before long he's convinced the men that he has been sent with thanks by the bakery as part of the jubilee celebrations. Soon the guards are laughing and slapping each other on the back, not noticing Zaini and me stalking up through the long grass behind them.

As we reach the wall of the palace, we crouch low and move towards the gate. I open the bottle and fish out two dream loops, one for each of the guards. Lalu and Mithi take one each, letting the loops hang from their beaks as they fly over to the guards and drop them softly onto the men's heads.

The dreams land like tiny, soft crowns, each the size

of a daisy. The magic takes its hold on them as soon as the threads melt in. Their eyes flicker a moment and one of them grimaces as he tries to fight the mind control, but the spell is too powerful.

I step forward. I am the controller and for an hour, if the spell has worked, these guards will do as I ask.

'We have come to clean the dungeon,' I announce. 'Let us in and do not mention us to anyone who passes by.' I have to stop myself from saying *please*.

The guards nod and one of them fumbles with his keys, unlocking the huge gate.

'Give me the keys,' I say, and he complies. I pass the huge keyring to Zaini to carry. It will help us escape if the spell of lucid dreams fails us.

'They are the king's men,' Kantar whispers softly. 'That's why their cloaks are blue. Red is the colour of the prince's guards.'

'Remain here and guard against any threat to the king,' I say loudly as they close the gate behind us. 'Do not trust the crown prince or his soldiers. They are traitors.'

'Yes, they are traitors,' one of the guards repeats.

Zaini and I leave Kantar and Rafi hiding in the shrubs on the inside of the gate and we continue down to the palace and the dungeon. I notice a pigeon landing on the wall by the gate as we turn to leave. It looks careworn and curious, reminding me of something or someone in a place I once called home.

The path to the dungeon passes through more long grass then dips down as it hits a wide, gravel courtyard. There are guards patrolling and prison staff coming in and out. Lalu has already taken another of the spells, which I signal to her to drop on the guard at the entrance, a woman with fierce eyes and a pole-straight back. As with the guards at the gate, the woman struggles as her mind comes under the spell.

We have used three of the spells, so I know I can't control many more people. I decide we will need to take this guard with us.

'Take us to the prisoners awaiting trial,' I command.

Her face clouds a moment then she nods. 'There are six prisoners.'

I clear my throat. 'Take me to Ibrahim and Selina Malou.'

She nods and leads us into the dungeon. A red-cloaked soldier passes us and looks at me intently then he turns to the guard escorting us through the prison.

Zaini looks at me anxiously. 'We need to get out,' she whispers, but I give a slight shake of my head. I'm not giving up when we have come so far.

'Why are you bringing underage prisoners into the dungeons?' he asks the guard.

'They are with me,' she replies in a flat, monotone voice, and the soldier seems to accept her explanation and carries on his way.

We continue walking further inside towards a large iron door.

'I need to tell you something, it's important,' says Zaini, but I am too busy thinking of the next step to pay her much attention. She shouldn't be panicking when I need strength. I wish Rafi had come instead, but he was right: the two of us together would be a risk. We'd be easier to recognize.

The guard unlocks the iron door, and it gives a long metallic groan as she pushes it open. Inside is a shadow-cast inner courtyard. Pale faces turn towards us with wide-eyed wonder and my heart soars as I see the two people I have come so far to save.

As I run towards my parents, all my careful plans slip out of my head.

CHAPTER TWENTY-SIX

The Ravens Close In

Papa starts to run towards me but stops when he notices Zaini. Ma is there too, seated on a bench, looking half the woman I remember, her face thinner and her hair greyer. My heart patters along as fast as Lulu's as I tip-tap across the stone floor towards them, barely able to conceal my excitement, but Papa's face flickers with fear and he gives a tiny shake of his head.

He flicks his gaze to Zaini who has followed me in through the iron door. Then his eyes turn back to me in urgent warning. He purses his lips and shakes his head again.

It's a warning.

Keep away.

A raven flies across the courtyard. I look around, expecting to see Citadel dream technicians, but perhaps it was only my imagination and the black feathers are not glinting with dream threads but simply the sunlight as it seeps over the walls of the dungeon building.

'Mimi!' Ma cannot hold herself back and runs towards me, grasping me tightly with warmth and fear. Her face, and mine too, are wet with tears.

'You should not have come,' she whispers in my ear. 'There is treachery in Ratnagar – and you must stop your aunt.'

'I came to clear your names,' I say, clutching at her shoulders. I'm as tall as her now and see the frailty and tiredness a younger me would have missed.

'Mimi,' Zaini hisses, 'I wish we could stay longer, but we need to get out of here!'

Ma raises her eyes and looks at Zaini then turns to me with a soft, urgent whisper: 'This is a friend of yours?'

'More than a friend, I owe her my life.' Zaini shuffles her feet and points to the door.

Another raven, and this time I am sure I see its belly glowing red, and . . . and something in its beak. It is green and writhing.

'We need to go, now!' shouts Zaini and she leaves the courtyard without even looking back.

The raven drops the thread on Ma, and it burrows into her skin. She clutches her head and falls in a heap, writhing in agony.

Papa rushes forward and we cradle Ma's head, whispering soft wishes. I look around for Lalu, but she is nowhere to be seen. Instead, I see Mithi darting across the courtyard chased by two ravens and – too late – I realize we have lost control. The guard who was escorting us has returned with a dozen red-cloaked soldiers. She shakes herself, an evil smile crossing her face.

'Nice try, Mimi Malou, but we've been expecting you.'

'But you should still be under the spell of lucid dreams,' I say.

'My mind was ready for it, protected by something even stronger.' She laughs, patting me on the shoulder as if she can simply jest with me. 'You are not the only one from Ratnagar to perform dream magic.

A heavy bell starts to toll, and more soldiers pour into the courtyard.

'Take the others away. Leave the Malous here until she arrives.'

Everything around me seems to fall silent and in my head I hear her footsteps arriving.

Click, clack.

Click, clack.

A metal taste hits the back of my mouth and my skin prickles with fear. Aunt Moyna strides in, followed by Suri, who is pulling Kantar along by the collar of his shirt. Rafi is nowhere to be seen.

My insides go ice cold. I look helplessly from my father to my mother. I go to take out my dream hook, in case my aunt should try to capture my mind, but Papa shakes his head.

Zaini slopes back in through the iron door and walks over to Aunt Moyna's side.

I can barely breathe. 'What are you doing, Zaini?'

'I'm sorry,' she says.

We were betrayed.

We are trapped.

Aunt Moyna walks over to us, looking down at Ma with a smirk on her face. 'Well, this comes as no surprise. My sister-in-law did always have such a weak mind.'

I jump up angrily and push her away. I want to tear her eyes out, but strong hands pull me back. It's Papa and I take shelter in his arms.

'Not now, Mimi,' he says. 'Don't give them the chance to paint you as a criminal like they have done to us.'

Aunt Moyna's gaze sweeps past Ma and settles first on Papa then on me. 'Ah, Mimi. I had such hopes you would become my successor. Such promise! I thought perhaps you would break the wondrous incompetence my brother created in our dear Citadel. You silly girl. Why did you have to jump into all this mess with such determination?'

My stomach retches and I surge towards her again, but Papa holds firm.

Aunt Moyna wiggles her finger. 'Very naughty. Still, you coming here will help put an end to all my "Malou problems".' She points to Zaini. 'And thanks to that talented young orphan, we tracked you down with a dream creature I gifted her.'

My eyes widen . . . and then I remember seeing Zaini listening to the dream technician as they struggled at Mumbai station – *appeared* to struggle . . . the way he smiled when she escaped him – the way she wrote down my plan in the inn earlier and didn't want me to see.

She has been spying on us and dropping clues for my aunt!

Kantar gives Zaini a thunderous look. 'What happened to friends stay strong . . .'

'Through right and wrong?' I finish.

'They threatened my little brother,' says Zaini, with tears in her eyes. 'I had no choice. And they promised me money. Enough for me and Avi to go to school and live like normal kids.'

'Lock them up!' says Aunt Moyna.

Papa, Ma, Kantar and I are seized and pulled by rough hands out of the courtyard. I try to keep close to my parents, but they are put in handcuffs and taken into a holding cell, ready for their trial tomorrow.

'Say your goodbyes,' Suri says to me. 'You will never see your parents again.'

I spit at her face, and she slaps my cheek. It burns and feels red, but I force myself to calm my rage. If I am to unpick this mess, I need a clear head and cool emotions.

'I will never forgive you, Zaini,' says Kantar. 'Mimi helped us to dream again.'

Zaini looks away in embarrassment. She doesn't see what Kantar does next. Secretly, furtively, he slides

211

something into my pocket. It's the keys – and he's stolen them from Zaini right under my aunt's nose. He isn't even looking at me, and I hold my breath, pushing down the hope that we might still be able to escape, willing it not to show on my face.

CHAPTER TWENTY-SEVEN

An Old Friend Returns

Kantar struggles and lets out a string of insults to the guard as we are pulled away. Phrases and exclamations that might colour my parents' judgement of him, but I can see what he is doing. It brings distraction and I use it to scan our surroundings.

What I see fills me with heavy dread, and my last seed of hope is blown away. Five heavy metal doors stand between the dungeon entrance and the cell we are taken to. Each has at least one guard posted on it.

As the final door is bolted and locked, we are thrown a piece of bread each and passed a jug of water through the bars.

'That's your meal for today, courtesy of Prince Sakim,' says a guard with a laugh.

The cell is clothed in shadow, except for a narrow beam of sunlight falling through a small, barred window, no bigger than a porthole, high on the wall behind us.

'I guess dream magic isn't always enough,' says Kantar, looking down at a beetle disappearing into a crack in the wall. 'Not when we are so few and they are so many.'

I push one of the hard benches under the window and stand on tiptoes, but my eyes can barely see over the sill. Outside the world carries on and, in the distance, I can make out marquees and stalls set up ready for the jubilee ball. I feel sick as I think of the people of Ratnagar celebrating a king they love, not knowing he is being poisoned to death with nightmares.

'Where is Rafi?'

'Soon after you left, the two guards at the gate seemed to come out of their spell,' says Kantar. 'I guessed Rafi would send you a signal and might also be able to use dreams in a way I can't, so I let them catch me while he got away.'

'Thank you,' I whisper, feeling heaviness at how my hopes and plans have not just failed, but have even made things worse than they were before. I carefully pull the keys from my bag and fumble through them. None of them looks big enough for the cell door.

'They probably have different ones for the inside and outside locks,' I say.

The sound of footsteps comes skittering along the stone floor outside. They seem lighter and quicker than a guard's, but not as clickety-clackety as my aunt's, and then my hopes are lifted further as the pigeon I saw before returns, along with its human.

'Madame Frenegonde!' I run to the iron bars and put out my arms.

She has come with a guard, who opens the door to let her in then leaves us.

'How did you find us?' I ask her.

She sits me down and pats my arm. 'I followed you. I must confess I have been worried about goings-on in the Citadel for some time.'

My face goes pale. 'No offence, Madame Frenegonde, but if you could follow our tracks all the way here, then I'm not surprised my aunt trapped us so easily.'

She laughs softly. 'No, I am not so nimble as to follow you directly. Do you remember the dream globe? We can use it to track dream creatures on the map in the Citadel. Lalu and Mithi led me all the way here,' she says.

A prickle of worry itches the back of my neck. 'How could you? The globe is stored in my aunt's office.'

'Your aunt was not in her office, a little like the time you were in there.' Madame Frenegonde smiles.

My worry softens a little. 'Thank you, Madame. You are truly kind – kinder to me than the aunt who was meant to be my guardian. I hope she is found out for the traitor she is,' I say. 'I hope someone tricks her and she is the one imprisoned without hope.'

'Hush, Mimi. Your aunt was not always so bad,' she says.

I remember how much Aunt Moyna cared for me as a young child, and how she would sneak me sweets and dream threads to make me laugh. Then she changed. I never understood why, but I know now. I remind myself why I am here.

From the corner of my eye I spot Kantar shaking his head.

'She betrayed Mimi's parents,' he says.

Madame Frenegonde nods slowly, her eyes misty with long-forgotten memories. 'It's true. Moyna was obsessed with building bridges with Ratnagar. With all its power as the largest city of the Northern Kingdoms, it was an important trading partner. Then when your parents stopped her talking to the prince, she wanted them out of the way. She wanted to restore the Citadel's wealth, but in the end hunger for success turned to greed and she fell into the clutches of the prince's evil plans.'

'She chose to help him,' I say. 'She created potions to terrify, to control, to murder. What good there ever was in her has gone.'

Madame shakes her head. 'Dear Mimi, you are still young. As you grow older you will learn that things are not always as black and white as they seem. I agree that your aunt has now become a dangerous individual. But I am not here because of her. I am here for me. Moyna is not the only one to have committed acts she might later regret. I have too, and it is time for me to pay for my misdeeds. I am going to get you out.'

My eyes widen. 'How do you plan to do that?' I don't have time to ask her what misdeeds she means.

'Money talks,' says Madame Frenegonde. 'These guards are poorly paid. I reminded them that you are children. I have told them I will return you to the Citadel and keep you in safety there to await your aunt. Some gold and a few choice dream threads helped convince them.'

Kantar frowns. 'We had keys. Look!' He pulls out the keys he took from Zaini's pocket.

Madame Frenegonde glares at him. 'Do you think you would pass each locked door unseen? Come with me if you want your parents to live, Mimi.'

As we follow Madame Frenegonde through the dungeon, Kantar keeps back a little. 'Don't trust her,' he whispers to me.

'I am learning,' I say. 'Never rely on an adult to do a child's job.'

In the courtyard outside the dungeon, a cart and driver are waiting for us. We climb up beside Madame and set off. The swirl of questions I had held in rushes to my mouth and Madame Frenegonde seems taken aback as I question her story.

'You said you have also done wrong,' I say. 'What did you mean? Did you know about my parents being innocent?'

She gives a slight nod and looks down. 'I did much to be ashamed of, and some of it put your parents in danger.'

I scream and stand up, ready to throttle her, to jump off the cart, to run away, but before I can do any of those things she grabs my hand.

'Wait,' she says, her eyes wet with tears. 'I'll make this right. There is a ball tonight and you need clothes. I will help you find a way to King Ganipal.'

I clench my jaw. 'How can I trust you now? My parents have been locked away in a dungeon for two whole years.'

'It wasn't supposed to be like this,' she says. 'They promised me it would be quick, and no one would be troubled, but they lied.'

'*You* lied to *me*, for two years! How could you?' I say, barely able to control my voice as we start to enter the town. Crowds pass beside us.

'I had no one to turn to, nothing I could do – please, let me help you.' She pulls out a money bag and thrusts it towards me.

'We don't need your money, Madame,' says Kantar. 'We can work out our own way in.'

Her face falls. 'I am sorry, but I understand,' she says, and she slows down the cart when we reach the town square.

'Goodbye, Madame. May you have luminous thoughts,' I say.

'And may your dreams shine ever brightly, dear children,' she says, tapping her head as she takes her leave.

Kantar is silent, simmering. 'She reminds me of my stepmother before she threw me out,' he says after a while. 'I don't trust her. Not one little bit.'

CHAPTER TWENTY-EIGHT

Time to Party

'If we want to blend in with high society, we need to look the part,' says Kantar. He points to a fancy clothing store, where mannequins pose in brightly coloured dresses and traditional clothing. My mouth falls open as he waltzes in and pulls out some outfits: a bright orange dress for me and a couple of cream silk shirts with Nehru collars for himself and Rafi. He slips them under one arm and then takes another random couple of outfits from the shelves.

A bespectacled shop assistant looms up from behind a clothing rack. She wears a flaming-pink sari, embroidered trailing orchids along its hem.

'Your outfit is beautiful,' I say.

She smiles but looks at the clothes in Kantar's hands and scrunches her nose.

'Can we try these clothes on?' he says, holding out the two outfits he picked last. 'My sister and I are going to a family wedding this weekend.'

The woman pulls her glasses down her nose and peers over them at Kantar with pursed lips, then she looks at me and then back at him.

'You certainly don't look like brother and sister.' She leans towards us and sniffs. 'And I suspect you have no means of paying either.'

My face flushes. 'We can pay,' I say, but the woman widens her eyes as she looks at the paltry loose change in my purse.

'Out!' she says firmly. She points us to the door and grabs the clothing from Kantar's hands. A security guard is summoned, but we scoot out before the man reaches us, and lose him as we meld into the crowds outside.

Kantar lifts the hem of his top. Underneath are the bright silk clothes we first picked out.

'Kantar! It isn't right just taking things like that,' I say.

'We can return it afterwards, so it's not stealing, it's borrowing, and it's for a good cause too.'

We take turns to go into the washrooms in a nearby restaurant and change into our party clothes. I tuck our old clothes down into my bag.

'How do I look?' asks Kantar. He rests one hand on his hip and swipes his other hand through his hair. 'Proper high society, eh?'

'You look great,' I say, trying a twirl that isn't quite as glamorous as I'd hoped. My shoes are still my black leather school shoes from the Citadel, but after all the travelling and hiding in rough clothes, it feels nice to be wearing soft silk clothes again. The comforts I took for granted in the Citadel seem a world away, but all the troubles I've been through since leaving make me determined to get back there and stop my aunt from destroying it.

'When this is done, we'll go to Juhu beach,' says Kantar, 'you, me, Rafi and . . . and all the other kids.' A flicker of sadness crosses his eyes.

'I'm sorry about all the trouble I've brought. I know you and Zaini were close.'

'I'll be okay,' he says. 'It was just, you know, I trusted her. We always took care of each other.'

'Join the club. I've been betrayed by my aunt for the past two years.'

222

'People are weird,' he says. 'I hate the lot of them.'

'Not me?'

'No.' He smiles. 'Not you, just the mean ones and the liars. Mostly the adults.'

'My parents are nice,' I say.

Kantar shrugs. 'Maybe, though your dad seems a little scary.'

It's my turn to smile. 'Trust me, my mother is worse.'

'I wonder what the king is like,' he says next. 'I hope we get to him in time.'

I check the clock in the market square. It's nearly six o'clock. Rafi could be searching for us, but he won't be looking for two children dressed in fine silk clothing all dressed up for a ball at the palace.

'Find my friend,' I say to Lalu. 'Rafi is somewhere in the city and Mithi will be with him.'

Lalu darts up, up, up above the market stalls then hovers over a corner on the opposite side of the square. When she zooms back to me, she has a chiffchaff on her tail and the two of them do a merry dance across the sky as they lead Rafi towards us.

He doesn't see us at first and walks past but turns and yells in happiness when I tap him on the shoulder.

'Such style! Very swish. I love the colour.' Then his

face clouds with the memory of our failed escape. 'I'm sorry, Mimi. I guess your parents didn't get out.'

Kantar spits on the ground. 'We were betrayed by Zaini.'

We tell Rafi about how Zaini was lured into betraying us.

'I can't hate her for what she did, she's got her brother to think of,' I say, 'it just makes me hate my aunt even more. But we still have to get to the king and save him ourselves. He's the one who still has the power to have my parents released. If he dies, the prince will surely have them judged as traitors and got rid of.'

Kantar nods. 'The baker told me the rulers of the other states around Ratnagar respect the king, but the prince – not so much.'

'They might find themselves targeted if the Citadel starts making nightmares for him. I reckon he'd start using it on all his enemies,' says Rafi.

Kantar passes Rafi the final outfit we 'borrowed' from the clothes store. He puts on the Nehru jacket as Lalu and Mithi skitter through the air above us.

'Right, we need to get into the palace,' says Kantar.

'Oh! Check *that* out.' I point to the queue of carriages bringing guests from out of town.

An over-excited socialite passes us by. As usual, being an important grown-up means she doesn't notice a group of children hanging around. She doesn't notice Rafi slip his hand into her bag, but she will certainly be disappointed soon to find her invitation is gone. We peer at the exquisitely engraved card.

The Royal Chamberlain is
instructed by
His Royal Highness the
Crown Prince Sakim,
Viceroy of Kalanaat,
Commander of the Palace Guard,
to invite
Mr and Mrs Suchi and Family
to a celebration of King Ganipal
the Third
on the occasion of his Silver
Jubilee,
at 6 p.m. on 31 December

'We can bluff our way in,' I say.

'It will be dangerous, and they know you are in town,' says Rafi.

I clench my fists. 'We have no choice. Besides, look at us!' I gesture to our outfits. 'They can't turn us away. Come on, let's go.'

The prince is hosting a party and we have an invitation.

CHAPTER TWENTY-NINE

Games and Distractions

We hear the palace before we see it.

Trumpets and dhol drums. Crowds and performers. It is a colourful, noisy spectacle and we sense the splendour of it from right at the bottom of the Royal Mall. The palace sits at the southern end of Ratnagar, where the streets get wider and the houses larger. A long road rises up the mountainside towards the white, marble-clad palace surrounded by ornamental gardens. Sweet rosebushes clamber up its walls and soft jasmine droops over its roofs. This evening, the path is lined by flaming torches and, behind them, soldiers hold back the townsfolk who have come to marvel at the spectacle and gaze at the rich and powerful guests invited to the ball.

'Hey, you three!'

We stand straight as pins as one of the soldiers ambles towards us. His cloak has a golden badge with a crown emblazoned on it. He is a round-faced man with his hair and beard oiled and combed to perfection and he pulls himself up on his toes a little when he realizes Kantar is slightly taller than him.

'Who are you? Show me your invitation,' he demands.

I hold my chin up, trying to look more confident than I feel, fumbling in my pocket and pulling out the invitation. Lalu wants to come out and examine the crowds gathered around the palace, but I calm her down and she stays hidden for now.

'We are the Suchi children,' says Rafi.

The soldier raises his eyebrows 'The Suchis of Savalpur? I thought their children were all grown up.'

'We're the younger ones. We were adopted,' I say. 'All of us. Mother and Father couldn't bear to have an empty home when the older ones left so they took us in from the street. Such kind people.'

'*Very* kind,' says Rafi, and Kantar waggles his head in agreement behind him.

The soldier scratches his chin and looks up as he

thinks about this. 'Where are your adoptive parents in that case?'

Kantar shuffles behind me. 'I don't think this will work,' he whispers.

'*Shh!*' I hiss from the corner of my mouth.

'Sir, our parents are already inside,' says Rafi. 'Surely you know that? They put their names on that list . . . See there?' He points to another soldier, who has a long parchment scroll he is using to check people in.

'Wait here,' says the soldier as he goes off to confer with his colleague.

Rafi nudges me. 'We need a distraction. Any ideas?'

I nod, though I'm filled with a prickly sense of danger. This might be the king's palace, but it is also the crown prince's lair.

Behind the palace walls are tall banyan trees with monkeys jumping in between them. I wonder if they can be tempted down to help us.

I touch my dream creature. 'What do you think, Lalu?'

Before I know it, my brave little hummingbird is darting in among the banyan trees in a haze of blue, causing the monkeys to shriek with delight and excitement. As she flies back to me, a couple of them try to catch her. They jump down from tree to wall and then into the palace grounds, barrelling towards me. I hide Lalu in my hair just as the monkeys become an unexpected part of the entertainment.

'Help!' cries a grand old lady playing tug of war with a monkey who appears determined to seize her silky silver scarf.

The soldier rushes over to help the lady retrieve her belongings. He swipes at the monkey, but neither side is letting go. The woman pulls on one end of the scarf, her face red with determination. The monkey tugs on the other, his teeth bared and growling. Each of them is a vision of determination, but neither will give way. The soldier grabs the old lady round her waist, puffs out his round cheeks and pulls too, but suddenly there's a ripping sound, the scarf splits in two, and the woman tumbles backwards, falling on top of the soldier. The monkey shrieks and screeches, and scarpers away, the scarf tucked under his arm.

Crowds have gathered to watch the fun, but we have already taken our chance, scuttling towards the inner palace gate while the round-faced soldier rubs his knee and pulls his cloak straight again. He looks around for us, but we tuck ourselves inside the main gate and continue into the palace.

I smile up as we pass the monkey, perched high in the banyan tree, tugging at the scarf and playing with the sequins on it; but I feel a twinge of guilt when I spot the poor flustered owner being escorted to the ladies' powder room.

The inner courtyard of the palace is filled with scores of entertainers – acrobats, fire-eaters and magicians doing card tricks. Strings of fairy lights are strung above our heads. None of the entertainers seems interested in children, so we skirt the walls and head towards the palace doors, avoiding ladies in dainty sandals and heavy-booted men, all desperate to show how rich and important they are.

Rafi and Kantar help themselves to bites from passing trays of food as I try to blend in, walking with a sure step, getting a feel for the layout of the palace, and all the while keeping an eye out for my aunt.

On the other side of the courtyard is a vast hall. Several corridors lead off it, and there are large, carved wooden doors with golden door handles too, and guards stationed two apiece in each corner. Two grand marble staircases arch upwards, coming to an embrace on the first floor, where the landing leads to even more passageways and even more doors. The palace is huge. It must have hundreds of rooms – and the king could be in any one of them. My heart sinks a little and I feel dizzy at the prospect of ever finding him.

'What does the king look like?' says Kantar.

'Dark eyes, dark beard,' says Rafi, 'just like ninety per cent of all the men here, except he has a crown.'

'What about the prince?' I ask.

'Same.' Rafi laughs. 'Except he doesn't get to wear the crown until he is king. In other words, not until his father dies, which I very much hope will not be happening for a long, long time.'

A ripple of fear catches the edge of my mind as I hear her.

Click, clack.

Suddenly everything slows down.

Click, clack.

Slowly, carefully I turn my head to see Aunt Moyna teetering across the hall, talking to Jamal. They turn down one of the corridors leading off the hall.

I chew my lip. Time is running out. 'We need to get to the king before she does.'

Kantar points to a clock on the wall. 'Let's split up, see what we find, then meet back here in an hour.'

Gently, I lift Lalu into my hands. 'Go look, little one,' I say, and stroke her head as she flies off in a buzzing blue blur.

I set off down the corridor after my aunt. I hear voices further ahead of me and spot her coming back towards me, following in the footsteps of a man who is a head taller than her. His nose is in the air and his robes are even more sumptuous than Jamal's. He has dark eyes and a bearded face but no crown. I turn away from them towards the wall, and pay close attention to a painting of the old queen.

'Your Highness, it is such a pleasure to finally meet you,' says my aunt in her high-pitched, pretend-friendly voice. My face flashes red with anger so I turn away and they don't notice me as I pretend to pay close attention to a painting of the old queen on the wall.

'It's not working, Moyna. Your potion is *not* working,' hisses the prince as they stride through a doorway into a drawing room. I catch a glance through the still-open door and see the prince sit down at a desk while my aunt waits in front of him. It must be very hard for her to be so polite to someone like him. A guard comes to stand at the door and scowls at me, so I scuttle away as he pulls the door shut and I move along until I find

Lalu at the foot of a stairwell. She flutters up the stairs then circles back, waiting for me. I make a start to follow her up when a voice rings out.

'You, child, where are you going?' A woman in an apron carrying a tray of tea and sweet cakes is coming down the stairs.

'I'm sorry, I seem to have got lost.'

'Party's out there –' She gestures in the direction I've come from. She has a kind face which is marked by years and worry. Her hair is tied back in a thick bun.

'Nice snacks you have there,' I say, trying to do the talking thing Kantar is so good at.

'From the best bakery in town, but he won't touch them,' she whispers.

'Who could refuse something so delicious?' I ask.

'The king. Poor thing, he hasn't eaten in days and barely takes a sip of water. Something's very wrong, I just know it. Anyway, I'm speaking out of turn. Sorry, Miss . . .'

'Suchi,' I say, not wanting her to think another Malou has come to do harm to her king.

'The kitchen staff will gladly eat what he turns away, though I do wish I could find something to tempt him.'

'Perhaps you will let me help. If I may?' She looks

234

confused but I take the tray from her as Lalu drops a thread of dreams on her and she sits down, a big smile on her face.

I make my way with the tray to the floor above and pass along another corridor where state rooms sit empty, following the blurred blue haze of my dream creature. She disappears into a room at the end of the passageway. The curtains are drawn, and the room feels abandoned. Much of the furniture is covered in sheets and those pieces that aren't have a thick layer of dust over them. At any moment, the prince or his red-cloaked guards could appear.

'Lalu, there's no one here,' I whisper urgently, but then I hear a rasping breath.

I poke my head through the open doorway.

'Stop, please leave me,' says a weak voice.

I take soft steps into the room, ears alert. Behind a carved wooden screen, I come upon an old man sitting in front of an empty fireplace. He has a crown on his head, a golden chain around his neck and a book in his lap. It is the king, but he is so weighed down by his symbols of power, he can barely lift his head.

He is a pitiful sight. I wonder how a man so mighty can be so sick and so alone. Perhaps the crown prince has already seized so much of his power that he has isolated his father and removed what little protection he had.

A faint scent of neglect and decay catches at the back of my throat. The room is in sharp contrast to the sumptuous, colourful splendour of the rest of the palace. With an unsteady hand, I reach out and touch the king on his shoulder. He shakes then starts moaning and jerking, as if in pain.

'Your Majesty, I am here to help you,' I say.

The king's eyelids flicker then he stills again, his breaths short and sharp.

I touch his shoulder again. 'King Ganipal, you and I have been wronged by people we trusted. Your life is in danger. Our homelands are at risk. I fear my people will fall into ruin too, and we have a common enemy.'

He utters a soft moan. Then he shudders, opens his eyes wide and sits up facing me. His eyes are open but his gaze is blank, as if I were a ghost. He looks straight through me.

'Your Majesty?'

The king's face contorts. 'No!' he shouts as thin shadows creep across the whites of his eyes. 'Please, stop! Let me sleep in peace.' He falls back on his couch, unconscious.

CHAPTER THIRTY

Sinking into Darkness

I hold out Lalu, who is glowing brightly, and she flutters above the head of the king, singing dreams that scatter over him like glowing rose petals. Pink and gold coiled threads sink into his skin bringing colour and life back to the dying king. But the nightmares will not give in so easily. They surface, angry and green, and rush to meet Lalu's dream threads. As they rise up, the king's skin becomes a mottled surface of pink, gold and black. A battle rages under the surface as the nightmares fight and curse, slashing the dreams into thousands of tiny fragments, and though the dreams shine brightly, they are no match for the anger and rage in these nightmare threads. Within minutes, Lalu's dreams melt away before they can ever sing their songs. The king moans and convulses as he sinks back under the clutch of the darkness stifling his mind and suffocating his life force. I wish I had more of the happiness dream thread Lalu and I took from the library when we were helping Rafi, but we used it all up to save him – and, without him, I wouldn't be here now. I need to think of something else. If I don't find a way to stop the king's terror, he will die. And, if that happens, my homeland, my parents, everything I wanted to save will fall into the greedy clutches of the prince and Aunt Moyna.

In desperation I shake King Ganipal's shoulders. His eyes flash open momentarily, and I gasp as a stream of nightmare threads cloak his eyes completely, turning them black as midnight. When he suddenly takes a sharp breath in and his head falls back, I stifle a scream.

With one hand I take out the bottle of nightmares I unleashed on the citadel guard and with the other, I hold my dream hook at the space between his eyes. I must extract the nightmares and destroy them in the light. They hiss and curse as my hook comes close, fighting hard to continue threshing the king's mind, but I hold firm and, fight as they will, my hook and the extraction spell draw them out of his mind.

'Come on,' I urge as they snuffle and crawl onto my hook. They sense my presence, and lift their tips to find me, hungry for a new mind to poison. I steady myself as they coil around the end of the hook and slide along its stem towards me, but I twist and turn the hook to gather the evil threads in a tight knot around the metal tip. When I can hold no more nightmares, I push the tip of my dream hook into the potion bottle and shake the threads into their new home. The threads scream and hiss as I tighten the stopper. When daylight comes I will destroy them in the sunlight, letting them fizzle and melt until they are gone, forgotten, as they should always have been.

King Ganipal takes a deep breath in and opens his eyes. This time, they are clear and focused. His mouth falls open at the sight of me and he sits up with a start.

'Who are you?' he asks. He shakes himself and reaches down to the ground to pick up his glasses.

I kneel. 'Sire, I have come to help you. Are you feeling better?'

'I don't know,' he says. 'I feel like I haven't slept in weeks.' His face is still pale and gaunt. Haunted. 'Why are you here?' he asks, looking at me with suspicion.

'You're not one of those healers my son has been bringing in from the Library of Forgotten Dreams, are you? Guards!' He coughs and falls back, exhausted. 'What is the point? The guards never come any more,' he sighs.

'Your Majesty, you are in danger, but not from me.' I flick my eyes back to the door. 'You have been poisoned by nightmares.'

The king splutters and his face reddens. 'How? We stopped the nightmare factory. I made sure of it – even though those traitors Ibrahim and Selina Malou tried to trick me into selling them again.' He frowns but then his eyes glass over and he starts to lose focus again.

I reach out and touch his shoulder. 'Please, Your Majesty, the Malous are my parents. They were betrayed, just like you.'

'You know nothing of Ratnagar,' he whispers.

I take out the coin I took from the bag of gold in my aunt's office, and his eyes widen.

'Where did you get that?'

'It is one of many, given to my aunt just last week, a payment for a commission of nightmares. Potions with your name on the bottle.'

'Nonsense,' says the king. His eyes look bewildered,

but I can see he's trying to think. 'You have no proof. Where is the bottle?'

I slowly pull out the bottle of trapped nightmare threads. When they sense the king's presence, they roil and churn, hissing curses that send shudders through me.

Ganipal looks at me wide-eyed. 'Who would try to poison me? I'm the king!'

'Your son, the crown prince . . .' I pause as he looks at me aghast. 'He sent an envoy to the Citadel. I saw him come with the bag of coins.'

'No, no, this is nonsense. Please go away,' says the king. He yawns. 'I'm tired.' He rests his head on the back of his chair. He looks like a baby bird, so alone and so vulnerable.

'Prince Sakim is meeting with my aunt as we speak. They intend to work together to re-create nightmares in the Citadel and use Ratnagar as a marketplace. Murderers and warmongers will return to your kingdom!' My stomach lurches as I see the king drifting into sleep. I shake his shoulder gently and he stirs. 'Only you have the power to stop your son,' I whisper. 'Please, let us work together for what we know is right and good.'

But I am about to discover that right and good are no match for evil when it comes in force. The king is weak, Lalu is out of dream threads, and thunderous footsteps come rushing to the door.

'Seize her!'

My aunt is here, together with the prince and Jamal and a whole retinue of red-cloaked soldiers.

CHAPTER THIRTY-ONE

The Crown Prince of Ratnagar

'Find my friends,' I whisper to Lalu, and she flees through the open doorway in a blue blur. My aunt swipes at her but misses. Aunt Moyna turns to me, grabbing my shoulders, her painted red lips twisted into a furious grimace.

'What is wrong with you, Mimi? You have put yourself in mortal danger by coming here.'

I push her away. 'You are the danger. You stand for everything that is wrong about the world. I won't help you and I won't be part of it.'

Aunt Moyna unclasps her bag and, as she reaches in, the sound of hissing, cursing nightmares drip out.

I back away towards the king, who recoils, childlike,

and clasps my hand. 'What is happening, Sakim?' he says to his son. 'I thought you were trying to find someone to help me, but this woman has brought poison.'

Prince Sakim pulls a seat over and sits next to the king. 'This woman is from the Citadel. She is one of the Malou family.'

'The Malous are in jail, and yet I continue to suffer the most terrifying nightmares.'

'Your suffering will come to an end soon, Father,' says Sakim.

I tug at the prince's sleeve. 'You must stop this. Look how weak he is already.'

'Silence!' says the prince, flashing an angry look towards me. Then he embraces his father, but when he pulls away his eyes darken.

'The Council of Elders will meet tomorrow, Father. You are too unwell to rule the kingdom.'

King Ganipal weakly protests as he tries to pull away, but his son keeps a tight grip on him.

'Sakim, what are you doing?' The king has tears in his eyes as he wheezes to catch his breath.

'The people need a leader, not a friend,' says Sakim.

As Jamal and the prince's men close in, the king looks

trustingly to them for aid. He can barely catch his breath and soon enough he realizes no aid is coming.

I watch helplessly as Jamal forces the king upright and my aunt pulls out the bottle I saw in the library. The writhing mass of night thoughts within it swirl and fight each other. They sense the king's mind is weak; they somehow know it is damaged and barely able to function, let alone fight back against their evil. They hurl at the glass to reach him, they hiss and scream, whispering malevolence, promising pain. I wince as I see the label: *Three drops for murder.*

The king twists and moans, but the hands holding him are too strong. The soldiers who surround him are like tigers closing in for the kill.

'Stop, this is not what dreams are for!' I shout, jumping onto Jamal's back, but he swats me away and I stagger back.

'Take her away,' says the prince, and I am pulled by rough hands towards the door. I struggle and shout, trying to get attention from outside, but the corridor is hopelessly silent.

As my aunt starts to untwist the lid, the low hiss and moans of the nightmares grows into a menacing thunder of voices, and the king holds his hands to his ears.

'Sakim! Jamal! Stop this! Stop it now, I am your king . . .'

The guards laugh, as does the prince. I pull free and run towards Ganipal, but it is too late. He sinks into a stupor as my aunt tips the nightmare over him. It crawls onto his face, working its way into him through his eyes, his ears, his nose, his skin, strangling his will to live; his love of life is being sucked away and smashed by these evil threads.

I scream in anger and dismay and then fear as my aunt looks at me with a cruel smirk. The bottle is not completely empty.

'No!' I cry, but my words turn to whispers as she walks towards me and holds the bottle over my head.

'I have failed you as much as you have failed me,' she says. 'I'm sorry.' Her voice sounds far away as she pours the final drop of the nightmare potion on me.

Suddenly everything feels slow and in between. In front of me, the soldiers' movements seem to grind to a halt. I gasp as the colour bleeds from their cloaks into the ground and turns into a puddle of blood. Their faces look at me blankly as they hold their swords aloft and the tips burst into flame.

Clink,

clink,

clink.

The metal tips of their boots ring across the floor as they advance on me, their eyes as red as the flames on their swords.

Help me! I shout, but no sound escapes from my mouth.

I try to run away, but the ground crumbles away beneath me.

My stomach turns over itself as I tumble into a darkness from where there is no escape. The soldiers float down and surround me, their cloaks like ragged wings that envelop me. I try to push away, to run, but my arms and legs are stuck. Unwilling. Unmoving.

I feel the burn of flame on my skin as the soldiers' swords swipe my skin.

One of them smiles with evil pleasure, revealing white, glistening, razor-sharp teeth.

I try again to scream but my mouth won't open and all that comes out of me are gargled moans.

At the corner of my eye, a flash of colour, and I try to reach towards it . . . azure-blue with flecks of gold and pink at the nape of her neck, skirting between the swords and the soldiers . . .

247

Lalu! It is my precious dream creature. I am in a nightmare of my aunt's making but poor Lalu has no dreams to save me. She flits around me, singing desperately, but she cannot counter the darkness. She fades away and I am alone.

I am falling into a cell, feeling cold. There is grime, sticky and fetid, under my hands.

This is just a dream.

This is not real.

I try to lift myself out of this nightmare, to believe it will end. My body cannot fight the suffocating darkness. My lungs feel on fire and desperate for fresh air.

I give up.

I have been buried alive in a circle of hell.

A low growl fills the darkness and I hear something shifting towards me. Something large.

I feel its breath sniffing at me. It smells of rotting meat and a drip of saliva falls onto my shoulder and I try to scream again, but once more my body betrays me and I am helpless in the shadow of a faceless beast.

I huddle into a ball. I am closing my eyes, waiting for the end, when my hand goes to my neck, where something is vibrating. My fingers brush against it . . .

If only I could remember what . . .

248

The pendant! Madame Griffin knew the dangers I was heading into. She tried to warn me, and her last words flood back into my consciousness.

It will bring you hope and light when none is left.

CHAPTER THIRTY-TWO

When All Hope is Gone

The pendant is calling to me. I feel the chain around my neck and force my hands up towards the capsule. It feels warm and hums gently as if it is alive.

I close my fingers around it.

The growl of the beast turns to a roar and a hot, large jaw scrapes my back. The monster knows my fears. It is playing with my mind as it closes in. Its breath is fetid and damp, it's mood is raging and ravenous.

With my last scrap of energy, I pull the two halves of the pendant's capsule apart and fall to the ground, my whole body shaking with exhaustion, but a seed of hope begins to swell. Inside the capsule are the threads of a ferociously powerful dream. They burst like fireworks into the darkness I am trapped in. These dream threads are beyond grade one. They are like sunlight and burn so bright I have to squint as I try to open my eyes. The threads encircle me and spike out towards the nightmare. The spirits of my parents, their parents and all my ancestors before me are in these dream threads and they are clothed in light and armed with swords which send bolts of lightning through the scene around me, ripping it apart. The ragged monster towering above me roars in pain as it is engulfed in flames of joy and hope.

I close my eyes and smile.
This is just a dream.
This is not real, and it will end.
The monster glows with the light of a thousand dreams and shatters into countless tiny fragments of light. My mind is lifted out of the cell and out of the darkness. I sit up and straighten my clothes as my aunt and the prince's guards look on in surprise. The explosion of dream light reaches the king, washing away all his nightmares as it did mine. I hold my breath as I watch the colour creep back into his skin.

Aunt Moyna leans over me, her eyes cold and distant.

'Take the girl to the dungeon cells. Let her join her parents.'

My body goes limp as the guards pull out handcuffs. After all I have done, I am alone. So be it. At least I will see my parents again. I think of my friends, Rafi and Kantar, and just hope they get away unseen.

As I hold out my hands to be led away, the door flies open, and there is Lalu, with Rafi and Mithi.

'Hang on, Mimi,' Rafi shouts. 'I'll bring help.' With that, he swerves between the prince's soldiers and races out of the room, his footsteps disappearing down the corridor. He is quick and the red-cloaks were taken by surprise. Two of them stumble out of the room behind him, but Rafi is gone.

Mithi and Lalu dart around the room, pecking at the prince and Jamal and the remaining soldiers. My aunt's creature, Kala, chases them, but this time he has no ravens to help him. He calls out in frustration, but my hummingbird and Rafi's chiffchaff are too quick for the koel, and he soon flags.

Rafi returns with Kantar, leading a chattering troop of monkeys from the banyan trees behind the palace wall, enticing them along with pieces of cake and other sweetmeats. The shrieking guffaws of the animals can't fail to draw the attention of more palace guards, and – finally – a group of blue-cloaked soldiers arrive. They rush immediately to their sickly sovereign.

'Seize this woman!' says the deceitful prince, pointing to Aunt Moyna, who still has the bottle of nightmares in her clutches. 'I found her attempting to assassinate my poor father.'

Aunt Moyna's denials and struggles are ignored. The bottle of nightmares falls to the floor with a thud as she is bundled away.

The king tries to sit up, raising his shaking hand to point an accusing finger at his son, but the cunning prince sinks to his knees, feigning confusion and compassion for his sickly father.

The soldiers hesitate, torn between the signal from their king and the forceful stance of his son. All the while King Ganipal's breaths are becoming more laboured again. He may be too weak to survive after all. The prince may still be king by tomorrow.

Not if I can help it!

I step forward. I clear my throat.

'Please, just listen to me. The king has been suffering from a nightmare potion, commissioned by the crown prince. Slowly administered, night after night, the

253

nightmares have weakened his spirit. Today was the final dose. It was delivered to the palace today –' I lift the empty bottle, which has the king's name on it and the fateful *Three drops for murder* – 'and was meant to kill him, but my friends and I, we managed to find him and block the nightmare in time. He will live.'

'Don't listen to her! She is but a child, and a liar at that,' spits the crown prince. 'Take these children away and deal with them,' he commands, pointing at Rafi, Kantar and me, and the guards start to close in on us again. Just then a familiar voice comes to our rescue.

'Mimi is telling the truth.'

It's Madame Frenegonde. She is standing beside Zaini, her orphan attire a grey smudge among the rich colours of the palace, I look at them with my mouth agape.

'The sudden assassination of a popular king would bring out many enemies,' says Madame Frenegonde, 'so instead a slow decline over years. Who would have questioned it when he finally succumbed to the darkness of sleep? You really did save him, dear Mimi.'

'Watch out Madame Frenegonde,' says the prince. 'Be careful what you say.'

'Do you know each other?' I ask her.

'Know each other? She is the willing tool of my father's decline. An ally of Moyna, she was the one who stole into his chamber and dosed him with a nightmare potion.'

'Is there no end to your treachery Madame Frenegonde?' I can barely speak for the rage in my chest.

'I am sorry, Mimi, but money is a powerful and persuasive reason to do things you don't agree with. I regret it now; I was foolish and greedy.'

I shake my head. 'I will never understand how you could willingly cause so much pain. The king, my parents, me . . . But I pity you and offer you forgiveness.' I turn to the king's soldiers. 'We must save the king. These people –' I sweep my hand round at the prince, his red-cloaks, Madame Frenegonde – 'are a danger to him.' The soldiers scratch their heads and look at each other, wondering whether to take the word of a mere girl over that of a prince. Some of them nod, others look to Sakim and Jamal, who move in like demons, and the king is too weak even to sit unaided.

I feel like there is nothing left in me. I have failed my parents and the Citadel, I have failed the king, and now my friends will suffer too.

Just then a red-flamed bird crosses the window.

'Tala!' I shout as the phoenix from the Citadel finds

us. 'You came!'

The blue-cloaks guard King Ganipal as Tala sings a beautiful dream to lift him out of any remaining nightmares. Slowly, Ganipal raises his arm. His voice is weak but as he points to his son one word – 'Traitor!' – falls from his mouth. He shakes his head. 'My heart is broken. Take him away, throw him in a cell and toss the key into a ravine,' he whispers.

The king's men ignore the arrogant protestations of Sakim, the disgraced crown prince of Ratnagar. They bundle him away with Jamal and the rest of the prince's guard.

Rafi and Kantar give Zaini a dark stare, but Madame Frenegonde puts her arm around our former friend. 'She helped me to find my way here. She has a knack for keeping hidden and, without her, you would all still be in a pickle. Please forgive her – she did what she did out of fear and desperation, and love for her brother.' Then she puts out her hands to a waiting red-cloak and is manacled and taken away for questioning.

More staff now make their way into the king's chambers, including a grand old man with a long staff and a thick grey beard. His wire spectacles almost slip off his nose as he bows deeply.

'Ah, my chief advisor, at last,' rasps the king. 'What have you got to say for yourself?'

'Your Majesty, the prince forbade us to approach,' says the man. 'Despite our concerns, he assured us he had your good health in mind and I regret to say we all believed him. It is clear, however, that rather than protecting you, he was sealing you in a royal prison, of sorts. Once you are fully healed, Sire, there is much court business to catch up on.'

King Ganipal waves his hand. 'Yes, yes. First, I want you to release the Malous. Next, a suitable reward must be made to this child for all she has done. Prepare a chest of gold and free passage to all my lands for her and any of her family – apart from her wretched aunt, who will be incarcerated.' With the nightmares gone, his face is becoming pinker, his eyes brighter.

I bow deeply. 'Sire, I did this for my parents and my homeland. By jailing my aunt and your son, you have saved not only your own life but that of many people in the Citadel.'

'Good, good,' says the king. He pats my head. 'Once you complete your schooling, you will always be welcome as a member of my court.'

'And if you please, Your Majesty, I could not have

done this alone,' I tell him. 'I would have tried but failed without my friends. Street children from Mumbai who have nothing, but who have given everything to help me because I am their friend.' Kantar bows, while Rafi plays the clown and does a curtsey-bow; Zaini shuffles awkwardly from foot to foot.

'Remarkable. Young orphans coming to the rescue of an old king. Thank you, children. This will be a story for the ages.' The king laughs softly. 'Oh, what a story we shall sing. We shall give you riches too, and a place to call home. Here, or in Mumbai, wherever you desire.'

My friends whoop, though Rafi is quiet.

'What's wrong?' I whisper.

'I want to try and finish my training at the Citadel.'

'Oh, yes, and you'll be the second-best dream hunter, right?'

'The *best*. Bar none.' He laughs and slaps my back.

The king clicks his fingers at his chief advisor. 'I feel I have been underwater, stuck in a dark, dangerous place for an eternity. I want colour, people, light and life! And bring the Malous to me; they too have suffered greatly.'

And with that, my friends and I find ourselves dining with the king in the great hall as we wait for my parents to arrive as free citizens at last.

CHAPTER THIRTY-THREE

The Way Home

The old factory of nightmares overlooks the train tracks passing through Ratnagar into the valleys and mountains beyond, and we gasp as we recognize it as the building we saw on our journey into the city. The paint is peeling, the windows are cracked and broken, and glass crunches underfoot as we walk through the abandoned building. The metal stairway creaks angrily as we make our way to a locked vault on the first floor where Jamal had been hoarding nightmare potions smuggled north from the Citadel. The king's guards break open the padlock and a grey glow leaks out. Garish, ghoul-filled nightmares in dark, stoppered bottles hiss and curse, trying to find their way out. To infest us.

The soldiers carry the bottles out into the sunlight, where they are opened, one by one, by my parents. The nightmares take many shapes: monsters, beasts, ghosts, all warped and fearful. They fight and scream but, in the end, as sunlight strikes them, they are splintered into powerless fragments. Forgotten nightmares. Once we are done, the builders will move in. The king has promised to refurbish the building and set up a new school for orphans in its place.

When the nightmares are no more, my parents and I are invited to an audience in the throne room.

When we arrive, I am taken aback by the grandeur of the room and magnificent riot of textures and colours. There is gleaming gold and soft silks, smooth marble and the glint of shining metals. There are courtiers in sumptuous attire, soldiers in beautiful blue cloaks, advisors and court trumpeters in rich velvets and brocades. It seems that the great and good of all Ratnagar and the Northern Kingdoms are here. King Ganipal is dressed in fresh robes and his eyes twinkle as he stands to greet us, signalling to his courtiers to do the same.

'My friends,' says the king, 'I hope, one day, you will

forgive me and my people for the wrongs my son has inflicted on you. Be assured that Ratnagar remains an ally of the Citadel behind the Mirrors.'

Papa stays silent for a moment, then he bows his head a little, pulling me and Ma close. It feels like he is weary of the world and the traps he has fallen into, but I grip his hand tightly and look up at him with a smile.

Everything is going to be okay.

'We will always help those who need it, Your Majesty,' says Papa. 'We have seen, as you have, that family bonds are not always what they seem.'

I think about Aunt Moyna. I hear she is in the women's prison, shouting curses to anyone who approaches her. I think her own nightmares have found a permanent residence in her mind.

'Long ago, Ibrahim, I learned to distrust the dream threaders,' says the king, 'those that took up residence here and started to craft nightmares. It was wrong and I tried to stop it. It seems my son disagreed with me. I should have trusted you when you and your wife came to warn me, but instead I listened to the snake-like whisperings of my son and Jamal and was powerless when they turned to the dark arts to remove me. We owe you a great apology, Ibrahim, Selina and Mimi Malou, for the wrongs you have all suffered.'

I clear my throat. 'Your Majesty, I would like, more than anything, to spread even more hope than before. Let our dreams heal the ailments of everyone, rich and poor. Money should not be the only reason we craft our potions.'

The king looks at me and raises an eyebrow. The room falls so silent I can hear my heartbeat thundering through my head. I hold my breath, waiting for the royal reply, and continue to look back at the king. His eyebrows wrinkle and his lips twitch.

Father grips my shoulder tightly, but I hold my head up high. I cannot let down those who have no voice.

I spot the edges of the king's lips curling upward and smile in relief.

'You, Mimi Malou, are brave,' he says. 'Slightly foolhardy, too, but a credit to your people. I am for ever indebted to you. Of course we should support what you wish. Dreams for all. Yes. Of course.'

A gentle stream of polite laughter ripples round the room.

'We will use my son's wealth to fund this work, in your name, and while we will never again allow nightmares to be sold here, from now on dreams may once again be traded and gifted freely in Ratnagar.'

Trumpets and tributes ring in our ears and I look around to capture the magnificence of the throne room one last time as the king leads us out and into his private rooms. He points to a mirror on the wall.

'Be back here at midnight and that mirror will return you to the Citadel,' he says, and I understand that our journey is almost done. It is the mirror that is directly connected to one in the Library of Forgotten Dreams in the Citadel, the looking glass Aunt Moyna used when she sent Madame Frenegonde into the palace to ply the king with nightmares.

My heart is still bruised by my old music teacher's betrayal, but at least she tried to make it right in the end. My parents took pity on her and have secured the king's clemency. She is banished from the Citadel but free to roam the world with her harp and her dream creature.

As for Aunt Moyna, I hear she veers between rage and guilt, confession and denial, but King Ganipal is determined she and the crown prince will remain till the end of their days in the same dungeons they once condemned my parents to. Suri has disappeared from the palace and a troop of guards has gone to search for her. She will have no friends left back in the Citadel, but I have a gnawing worry that my aunt may have allies who could use her knowledge and skills. My father promises we will leave no dream unchecked in our efforts to find her.

My friends and I play with the king's grandchildren. Princess Amara is the same age as me and tries to teach me how to dance. Lalu seems to like her and lets the young princess stroke her neck like I do. We promise to keep in touch, and she assures me she will keep an eye out for any more trouble from her uncle, Prince Sakim.

It is agreed that we will all visit Ratnagar again next summer. I promise the royal grandchildren I will teach them how to thread dreams and at bedtime they wriggle with delight as Lalu dispenses little dream threads over them before they are taken off to sleep.

As we prepare to leave, I take a last look out of the window, over the palace grounds. I spot a pigeon with glimmering feathers settling on the shoulder of an old lady wrapped in a long grey cloak. She raises her hand to me in salute.

'Goodbye, Madame Frenegonde,' I whisper.

*

Frost glints on the grass and the palace walls and the clock strikes midnight as we stand before the mirror, preparing to step back into the Citadel. My friends and I are all there, my parents too. My mother reaches for my right hand, my father for my left; behind us, Rafi, Kantar and Zaini hold hands too.

'And so, dear friends,' says King Ganipal, 'it is finally time for us to take our leave of each other. Are you ready?'

We nod, and I grip my parents' hands more tightly.

'May your thoughts be luminous,' says the king.

'May your dreams shine ever brightly,' we reply, and we step forward through the mirror and return home to the broken Citadel.

I walk past shelves of broken bottles in the library; there is sorrow, too, at what has been destroyed. 'So much history lost. I couldn't save them,' I say.

Ma wraps her arms around me. 'History is not just the past, Mimi. We create it, and we will keep creating it. The dreamers keep on dreaming, and they always will. As long as we have our dream hooks and mirrors, we'll be here to catch the threads before they are forgotten.'

My father seems an older man after all he has been through, and as he surveys the secure section, he shakes his head softly. 'I trusted my sister,' says Papa, 'yet under our own roof she deceived us.'

'I think she began by wanting to help the Citadel thrive but, in the end, she became snared in a web of darkness,' says Ma.

She is right. Aunt Moyna wasn't born evil. She loved me. Perhaps she still does, but she must pay for the vile scheme she was part of.

We walk into the courtyard. The council of the Citadel has reassembled for the first time in two years. They embrace us and ask forgiveness, but my parents brush their worries away. If my aunt could fool a wily old king such as Ganipal, what could the peace-loving librarians of the Citadel have done to stop her?

Madame Noori taps her stick on the ground and the ceremony begins. 'Since the founding of the Citadel, the dream creature Tala has symbolized our peace and continuity. Passing from generation to generation, she is the companion of the head librarian. Our guardian. Tala's refusal to become Moyna Malou's dream creature was significant. It exposed Moyna's claim to be rightful heir to the Citadel as a lie.'

A chorus of murmurs. Then shouts, as fingers point to the sky. A red dot circles above us, slowly, majestically, round and round, descending from the mountains above the Citadel. We watch with wonder as the dot comes closer; a fuzzy haze of red becomes a glorious firebird. Tala the phoenix, her dazzling red tail feathers trail behind her as she swoops down and lands on my father's arm. My parents bow their heads to Tala, and she returns their gesture with a squawk and nuzzles my mother's cheek.

'Tala always preferred you,' says my father, only half joking.

The crowd erupts in applause. Rafi, Zaini and Kantar are whooping louder than anyone. This is not just a dream creature but a mythical bird, carrying magical dream threads. The thought of Mumbai and the orphans waiting there reminds me: our group will soon be separated once again.

We gather in the head librarian's office, where Ma treats us to steaming cups of tea and a tiered tray laden with pretty iced cakes. Rafi races his way through them, making sure he has a spare cake in his hand whenever one is in his mouth.

I notice Kantar takes just one, slipping another into his pocket. His face reddens when he spots me watching him. Life has taught him to be prepared always for hardship and the next hurdle.

'For the others,' he whispers.

'Don't worry, we'll pack you a whole box before you go,' I say.

Papa clears his throat. 'You are all heroes to me. Rafi, Kantar and Zaini, you should never have had to endure the hardships of your life in Mumbai or the troubles thrown at you in Ratnagar. It is not a life any child should experience. And so we would like to make you an offer. Live your childhood here, in comfort,' he says. 'You and all your friends are welcome in the Citadel.'

Rafi wants to stay. He says he is keen to finish his training, and he has no family to go back to in Mumbai, but Kantar and Zaini remain silent and look out of the window. Apart from the last few days, they have never known anything other than the bubbling cauldron of the big city. As much as I know they are anxious to return there, my heart sinks at the thought of losing them.

'We'll be glad to visit you and all,' says Kantar, 'but we are children of Mumbai. It lives in us, the music, the food, the people.'

'Avi, my brother, is back there too. I need to go to him,' says Zaini.

'I understand,' I say, squeezing her hand, and she smiles softly. 'There is always a welcome for you and Avi and Kantar here,' I say, with slightly stingy eyes.

'And one for you in the city of dreams,' says Zaini.

I tug my father's sleeve. 'Papa, they must have somewhere safe to live. Just as the king promised.'

My father nods. 'I suspected this would be your choice, so I hope you won't mind that I have made arrangements for you with an old friend of mine in Songra.'

Zaini and Kantar look intrigued, and Rafi and I look at each other.

'Amir, the owner of the guest house?' I say.

'Yes,' says Papa. 'A fine man and an excellent dream crafter. Amir owes me a favour or two. What I propose, Zaini and Kantar, is that he and his wife will organize schooling for you and your friends in Mumbai. You can board there during term and return to the care of Amir and his wife in the holidays.'

Zaini nods but Kantar's face crumples in disgust. 'School? Why would I need that?'

My mother crosses her arms. '*Ex nihilo nihil fit.*' She spots our scrunched foreheads. 'It's Latin. Nothing comes from nothing, young man. I have great hopes for you, Kantar. A leader is what you are, and leaders

269

can change the world.'

'A "leader". I like that!' Kantar beams, and I think his eyes are a bit shiny too. Personally, I am not sure how long that feeling will keep him in school, but if I know my mother, she will be keeping her eye on him.

'I hope, one day, you will both come back and learn to read and write your own dreams into stories,' I say to Kantar and Zaini as we wish each other sweet dreams and head off to bed.

As I finally sink my head into the soft, goose-down pillows of my bed in the Citadel, I realize I no longer need to fear the night and the dark dreams that once haunted me. While I cannot yet forgive my aunt, I am not to blame for her actions.

Dreams, like stories, will always come to an end, but if I can help a single person come through their own personal nightmares, then the treasures in the library will not have been gathered in vain.

Dream Thread Classification

From *A Beginner's Guide to Dream Hunting*,
by Geeta Ganipati

Dream sequences are composed of myriad different thoughts and qualities. As they escape the mind, they fall into their constituent parts based on emotional content (the dream threads). The following is a guide to the five basic categories of dream thread, and how you can identify them. To recreate the complexity of an authentic dream, the librarians will concoct a personalized mix, so, for example, a grade three dream can be of as much value as a grade one dream, depending on the needs of the sleeper. When it comes to selecting and grading dreams, the following rules apply:

- Dreams are rarely straightforward and some qualities may span across different grades, so the average score should be calculated.

- Only grade three dreams and above should generally be used in dream threading.

- Grade five dream threads derive from nightmares and should never be harvested.

Grade one dreams

Often associated with joy (gold), playfulness (orange), friendship or belonging (yellow), these threads are classically a perfect helix in shape and demonstrate a playful curiosity, lifting their tips to sense both the sleeper and other dream threads. The energy they contain is demonstrated both by their movement, which includes rotation, folding and sideways motion and by the sparkle of each individual fragment of dream within. Sometimes mistakenly used to create potions of so-called 'amour', these dream threads are more likely to inspire childish pranks or embarrassing dance moves than professions of love, but all in all they contain concentrated happiness and are a delight to handle. A small amount of grade one thread is useful in any dream potion, to drive a positive and joyful narrative.

Grade two dreams

Representing dreams associated with success (silver), pride (purple) and steadiness (pink), these threads are ideal in potions seeking to provide courage and determination in hard times or encouragement for those who need inspiration to reach higher goals. The threads are slightly looser in form, taking a wavy appearance, but have creativity in their movement, often sensing other threads and forming complexes. They have a regular sparkle of energy and are a great addition to any dream potion, especially for those feeling low in spirit or of a nervous disposition. They are particularly useful for newly qualified teachers, doctors or athletes, but are not recommended for politicians or head teachers (where a good amount of intrinsic self-belief often already exists and may be propelled into autocratic tendencies). The silver is a perfect pre-exam pick-me-up to give pep to nervous students of all ages. It is advised to simultaneously dose parents with a pink-hued potion to help manage expectations.

Grade three dreams

We all need strength from time to time, and grade three dream threads present a perfect addition to any dream potion to support bravery, endurance and effort. They represent the steady workhorse of all our minds, supporting a good attitude to life, work and relationships. Blue in colour, these threads take a simple wave form, though their content and activity are anything but. The movement of these threads is described as curious. Intermittently it will take the form of bending and twisting on themselves. Rather like grade one threads, grade threes have a good sense of environment and sparkle occasionally but are less interactive than grade ones and instead focus on learning and improving their own content by drawing inspiration from their surroundings. They are ideal for inspiring productivity in those who are slightly workshy. The threads work well when mixed with a tiny snippet of a yellow grade one to encourage loyalty to the cause.

Grade four dreams

We start to venture into negative emotions with these sullen threads, which are consumed with anger at the world and disappointment in others. It is best to avoid these red threads in any dream threading, particularly for teenagers (or the parents of teenagers). Their form is simple, linear and they show minimal movement, preferring to lie still and sense the world around them. With little or no sparkle, they simultaneously generate and absorb feelings of injustice and this becomes apparent in the dreams they produce. An amusing experiment is to mix a grade four thread with a playful orange grade one. The reaction is sparky, though not particularly constructive.

Grade five dreams

These are dark, dangerous night thoughts and should not be harvested or stored. If caught in error, they should be bottled at arm's length and disposed of by the head librarian. They bring forth dreams full of fear, sadness, pain and dismay. Their behaviour is as aggressive and hurtful as the emotions they contain. They possess inverted energy, sucking away any positivity in the environment and replacing it with malevolence. Their movements are vicious and angry, and they will typically exhaust themselves fighting themselves and other types of dream thread. Avoid, avoid and, if in doubt, avoid.

Dream classification table

Grade	Colour	Shape	Movement	Sparkle	Energy
1	**Gold** (Joy) **Orange** (Playfulness) **Yellow** (Friendship/ Belonging)	Helical	Playful	Constant	Active – twist, fold, bend
2	**Silver** (Success) **Purple** (Pride) **Pink** (Steadiness)	Wavy	Creative	Regular	Responsive – mainly folding and bending
3	**Cobalt/Blue** (Bravery/ Endurance/ Effort)	Curvilinear	Curious	Occasional/ Variable	Intermittent – bending and occasionally twisting
4	**Red** (Anger/ Disappointment)	Linear	Minimal	Rare/ Barely visible	Sullen and silent, occasionally twisting
5	**Green** (Fear) **Black** (Hatred/ Malevolence)	Asymmetric/ Changing	Angry	Inverted	Aggressive – fighting, destructive

Acknowledgements

Writing a novel means many hours of solitude so I am immensely grateful to those who have enabled it, those who lifted me out of it when needed and to those who read my words and helped me shape a story ready to go out into the world.

My first thanks go to my amazing agent, Chloe Seager, who is simply the best advisor, mentor and champion, and whose ideas and plans are always worth following.

Arub Ahmed and Michelle Misra from Simon and Schuster presented me with a vision for my novel that showed they totally got what I was trying to write and have been wonderful editors. Thank you to Susan Hall and Leena Lane for copyediting and proofreading the work, Olivia Horrox, Ellen Abernethy and Jess Dean for their help in marketing and PR and to Rachel Denwood and Lucy Pearse for their enthusiasm and welcome to the Simon and Schuster author team.

The beautiful illustrations on the cover and throughout this book comes from the talent of cover designer Sean Williams and illustrator Federica Frenna whose visual interpretation of the writing really brings the story alive.

Leila Rasheed and Stephanie King deserve special mention for supporting my writing development with a Megaphone Writer's Scheme mentorship. I was lucky to be taken under the wing of prize-winning children's book author Maisie Chan who was so generous with advice and support.

Catherine Coe had a sparkle in her eye when she heard my idea for a story about dream craft, and thanks to the Arts Council UK I was able to work with her to pull the story into a novel which underwent further refinement during editing with the amazing team at the Novelry, where Louise Dean and Krystle Appiah helped me polish it and send it winging its way to Chloe. And so, the story comes full circle.

But this novel is more than just the words on the

pages of this book. Writers' groups are really important for nurturing the budding writer, and the ones hosted by Write Magic, Megaphone and Writementor have been a lifesaver for company, friendship and careful critiques. Thank you all, especially Iqbal Hussein, Munira Jannath, Alka Handa, Zareena Subhani, Abimbola Fashiola, Ten The Goi, Charlotte Tulinius, Daniel Hobden, Michele Helene, Sharon Boyle, Fran Webb and Ellie Salkeld.

To friends who read the raw novel and were so kind and constructive in their feedback - Camilla Salvestrini, Shruti Agrawal and Caroline Fonjock. You helped me cement the pace, structure and authenticity of my work whilst your enthusiasm healed many patches of self-doubt.

My family has always been there to support me (and to keep away when it came to deadline time). Thank you to Léon and Zahra for being honest critics and most fiercely supportive offspring a parent could ask for and to my parents who instilled in me a love of learning.

Finally, to Pierre who has always encouraged me to follow my dreams. To you and for you I am most thankful of all.